Sab

Witch

Contents

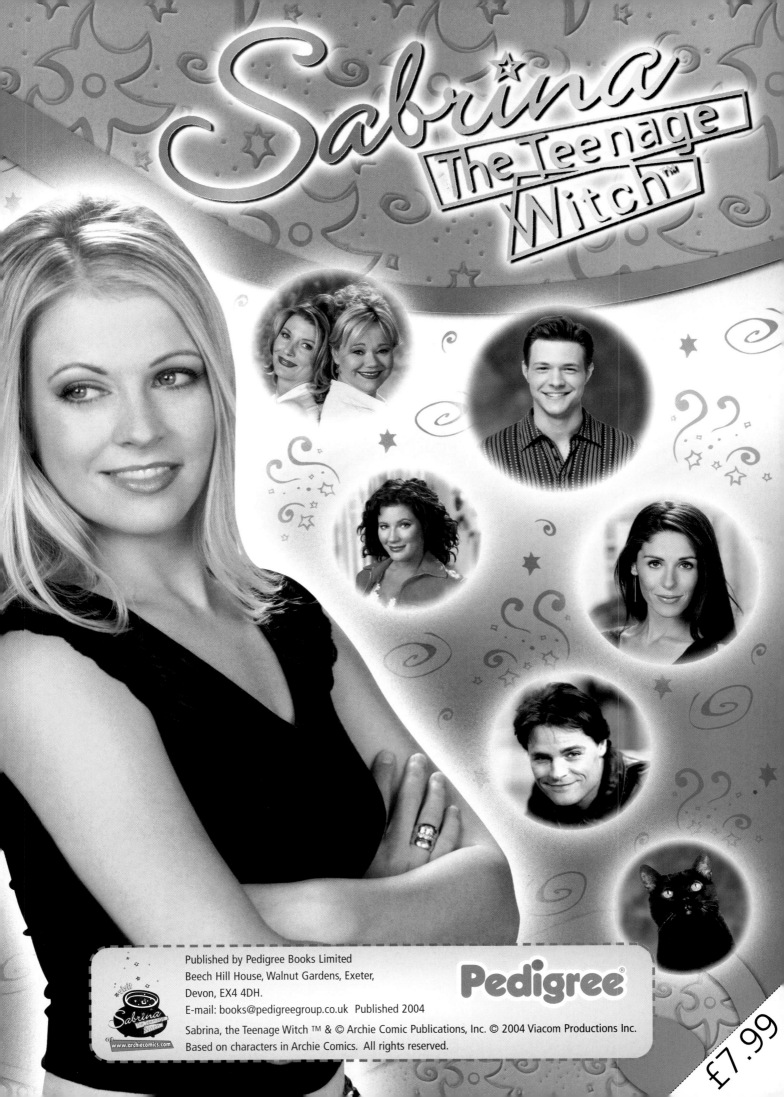

Sabrina The Teenage Witch™

Published by Pedigree Books Limited
Beech Hill House, Walnut Gardens, Exeter,
Devon, EX4 4DH.
E-mail: books@pedigreegroup.co.uk Published 2004

Pedigree®

www.archiecomics.com

£7.99

The Gang's

Hi, everyone! Boy, there have been some changes in my life since my last annual. I`ve left college, become a freelance writer and, as you will learn, I might even be getting married! Wow! But for those of you who don`t know me that well, here`s an update on my family and friends!

Sabrina Spellman

That`s me! I first got my witch powers when I turned 16, so apart from dealing with school, boyfriends and zits, I had to learn a whole new craft - witchcraft, that is! I`m much older now, but my spells still have a habit of going wrong! I used to live with my Aunt Hilda and Aunt Zelda, but after Aunt Hilda got married they left for a new life elsewhere in the universe. That was just about the time I`d finished college, so I moved back in to their house with my best friends Roxie and Morgan. Oh, and my talking cat, Salem!

Hilda & Zelda Spellman

My kooky Aunts, who taught me all I know about magic. Aunt Zelda is the sensible one, and a science genius. Aunt Hilda is slightly more wacky, but I love and miss them both so much. I don`t get to see them as often as I used to, but I know if I ever need them, all I have to do is call and they`ll be there in an instant. And I do mean `instant`! That`s the great thing about being a witch - you don`t have to rely on public transport!

Diana Spellman

My mom`s a mortal who's on an archaeological dig in Peru. I`ve only seen her once since I turned 16, but that isn`t her fault. When she married my dad, who`s a warlock, this so incensed the rotten Witches` Council that they enforced that stupid rule that if I saw her once I got my powers, she`d turn into a ball of wax! (Yeah, really!)

All Here!

Salem

He`s greedy, annoying, and a complete pain at times, but Salem is the best friend/cat a young witch could have (then again...). He`s always stuck by me...usually because he`s hoping there`s something in it for him! Salem isn`t really a cat - he`s a power-hungry warlock who got turned into a cat by the Witches' Council when he tried to take over the world! (And he`s still hoping to do it one day!)

Harvey

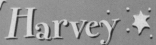

Ahh...Harvey...there`s a lot of history between us, all of it wonderful! We used to be an item, but now we`re just best friends. He still gets jealous of me seeing other guys though, (one guy in particular!) but he`ll always be there for me. Oh, yeah, and he`s the only mortal who knows I`m a witch!

Aaron

The `one guy in particular` I was just mentioning! It`s best to keep him and Harvey apart whenever possible! Our relationship has become very serious of late. Could Aaron be my one true soul mate? Read on and find out!

Morgan

My roommate and one of my best friends. Morgan is rather self-centred and conceited at times, but she has a kind heart. She`s working to become a successful fashion designer, which is great for her, because her looks and clothes are the only things she`s interested in!

Roxie

Roxie is my other roommate and other best friend - not exactly the optimistic, trusting type, but I'm working on her. She has her own daily radio talk show, a job Roxie really enjoys because she gets to tell people what she thinks and get paid to do it!

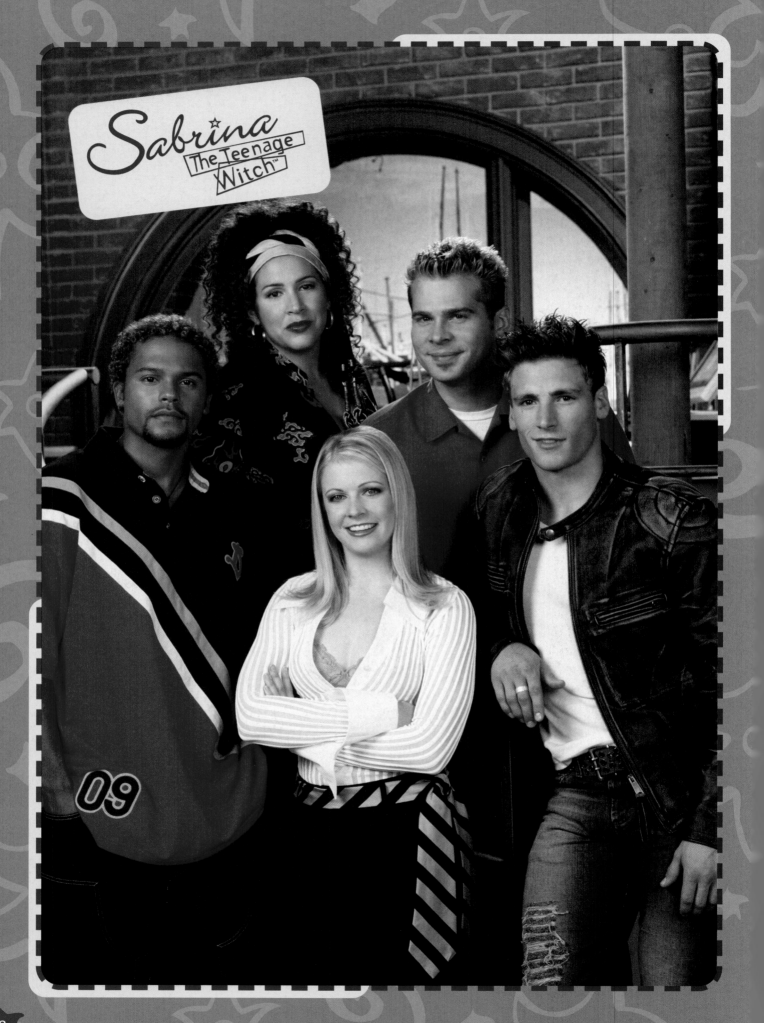

Total Sabrina Live

Hi guys! Sabrina here. Remember me telling you in last year's annual about what happens to witches who lose their life's soulmate? They freeze and fall to pieces. And that's exactly what happened to me!

Original story written by David Babcock

There I was at Aunt Hilda's wedding, being told by Harvey, my ex, Josh, my current boyfriend and Luke, the gorgeous guy I'd been flirting with, that they were all leaving me.

They walked out the door, and I then discovered that one of these guys just had to be my soulmate because...I froze...and fell to pieces! CRASSH!

So there I was, scattered over the floor of my Aunt Hilda and Aunt Zelda's kitchen in dozens of pieces, when Salem entered.

"Okay, I don't know what happened here," he said, jumping onto the table, looking down at the mess that was once me. "But a hundred bucks says I get blamed for it."

It was then that Harvey came back.

"Sabrina," he said. "Before I go, I want to say - -,". He looked down at the broken pieces and glared accusingly at, "Salem!"

Salem wailed. "Where is my bookie when I need him!"

Harvey knelt down, examining the pieces more closely.

"Wait a minute...this looks like Sabrina`s mouth...and these are her eyes..."

And then suddenly, I was magically restored to my old self again!

"Whoa!" I gasped, looking down at myself. "How did I get put back together?"

Salem and Harvey, who`s the only mortal to know I`m a witch, were speechless. But the answer became clear when Aunt Zelda appeared, slightly shorter and more youthful than the last time I`d seen her. In fact, she was an eight year old kid!

It seems the only way she could restore me back to normal was to sacrifice something of her own - her adult years.

"You call that a sacrifice?" snorted Salem. "I used to be a guy and now I have to poop in a sandbox."

My Aunts...always there for me.

I told Aunt Zelda that she really didn`t have to look after me, anymore. She and Aunt Hilda had taught me everything I know. I`d be graduating soon, and I was going to look for a job as a reporter.

Aunt Zelda knew it was time to let go.

"Goodbye, Sabrina," she said, hugging me. "And good luck."

"Wait!" I said urgently, before she disappeared by pinging herself away. What about

my true love? Will I ever find him?"

"Yes, but it may take you the rest of your life," she said solemnly. "Goodbye." And with that...she was gone.

* * *

So I was on my own, moving into my Aunts house with my roommates, Roxie and Morgan, and very soon desperately looking for a job. I`d already quit my part-time position at the Boston Citizen newspaper, wanting something more permanent, but no matter how

many resumes I sent out to national newspapers, no one seemed interested.

Morgan was having much more luck. She had won a writing contest at MTV, and had been selected to interview a rock band for Scorch magazine.

I later found out that she stole a writing sample of mine for the contest. Okay, a lousy thing to do, but I wasn`t angry - I was delighted. My work was being appreciated!

We went to the office of Scorch to find out more. Only my mouth opened before my brain kicked into gear. I told the reporters there that I was a writer, too.

"I mean, not this kind of stuff," I scoffed derisively. "Serious journalism." Oops. That didn`t go down too well. But hey. It`s true.

Anyway, Morgan was to go to New York and interview top rock band, Course of Nature, and she was allowed to take two friends with her.

Which was great news for me, and Roxie, too. I had recently sent my resume to the editor of the New York Herald Examiner, one of the biggest newspapers in the country. And Roxie wanted to sneak on a live MTV show to protest people eating meat. Roxie was always protesting something, and this was her chance to reach a huge audience.

So, with a little bit of magic to ensure my resume was on the top of the pile of job applications, I had arranged a job interview for the same time that Morgan was interviewing the rock band!

* * *

The next day, Morgan, Roxie and I were being driven around the streets of New York in a limo courtesy of MTV!

"This is so exciting!" squealed Morgan, as we passed the Empire State Building. Unfortunately, and unseen by me, Salem, who I had brought along secretly in my shoulder bag, accidentally fell out of the car as it was speeding along! He was lost - - in New York!

Arriving at the MTV studios, we were soon in the dressing room of the band, Course of Nature.

"So, like..." Morgan said nervously, addressing one of the band, after I had suggested she ask about his musical influences. "Who influenced you to cut you hair so short?" And the interview went downhill from there...

Meantime, poor Salem was in deep trouble. He found himself in a dirty back alley among stinking garbage cans and boxes, looking up at a huge, vicious New York rat. And trust me, some of the rats in this town can be the size of small dogs.

"Okay," gulped Salem nervously. "That is one big rat."

Let`s face it. The fat cat from suburbia didn`t stand a chance against the mean city rodent. SMACK! WHAACCK! WALLOP!

* * *

I wasn`t having too good a time, either. At the offices of the New York Herald Examiner, the editor told me that he thought I`d come about a secretarial job. My magic had put my resume on the wrong pile. Aggggh!!

I was out of luck, anyway. As much as the editor liked my writing style, he felt that I wasn`t mature enough, and had too much youthful

exuberance to be suited for the job.

"I resent that," I said. "And I resent you saying I`m not mature."

Just then, his phone rang. I snatched it up. "Mr Fleming can`t come to the phone," I snapped angrily. "He`s too busy being mean!"
I slammed down the phone in a huff and stormed out of his office. Smart move, Sabrina. That`ll impress him.

***

Luckily for Salem, we found him before we left New York. Back home in Boston, I bandaged his sore head and put some band-aids on his body.

"I got beat up by a rat," he groaned, feeling terrible. "He humiliated me."

"I`m sorry, Salem," I said, preoccupied with finding a job. "But I have bigger problems. Just butch it up."

And for once he listened to me, starting his own exercise programme to pump up those feline biceps.

Morgan was having problems, too, specifically writing the article for Scorch magazine. She couldn`t even find another word to use to describe the band other than `cute`.

"Hey, Sabrina," suggested Roxie. "Why don`t you write the article? You want to be a reporter. And it might get you published."

"I`ll write it," I told Morgan. "If I get the credit. No more fronting for you."

Morgan looked offended at this. "I would never take credit for something you wrote," she snapped. Then she blushed. "Twice in one week."

This, I thought, was my first step up the ladder to fame, fortune and success.

Annie, the editor at Scorch, soon burst that particular bubble.

Even though she though
the piece well written,
very professional
and very

well researched, she also thought it was very…bland! Not only wouldn`t she pay me for the work, she wasn`t even interested in publishing it.

"Anything printed in Scorch represents a certain point of view," she said, gesturing to her staff, Cole, James and Leonard. "These people have life experience. I`m guessing your life experience comes down to a junior high certificate for perfect attendance."

Boy, was I miffed! There had to be a way of getting myself noticed.

Watching Roxie watching a live pop music programme gave me the idea how. Roxie had left the room to get a snack and I was about to `ping` myself to the show`s studio when the newly buffed Salem came in. He was twice his normal size! And the vest and bandana he was wearing made him look very macho.

"Next time you`re going to the Big Apple," he growled. "Take me with you. I want to deliver a message to my friend, Ratso."

After magically `fixing` our television so that Roxie wouldn`t see what I was about to do, I picked up the cat and - PING!

Next moment we were in the TV studio. While Salem went off to give a rodent serious payback, I sneaked my way into the audience. When the host got close, I leapt out and gabbed the microphone from him and spoke directly to the camera.

"I want a job," I said bluntly. "I`m a journalist and I can`t find a job. All right, "I admitted. "I`ve gotten a few offers but I turned them down. Long story short, I`m an idiot."

***

While I was pleading for a chance to become someone's star reporter, Salem was back in the alley, confidently staring down the rat.

"All right, cheese-breath," snarled Salem, flexing his biceps. "It's you and me. Right here. Right now."

Suddenly, some garbage cans fell over with a CRASH! Salem thought the rodent had brought some of his friends along, but that didn't scare him. He could take them all on.

Only it wasn't a bunch of rats...it was an alligator! A very big, very mean alligator.

It bore down on Salem, menacingly snapping its jaws.

"Please," squealed my terrified, yet vain kitty. "Not the face!"

* * *

Back at the TV studios, I had just one more thing to add.

"There`s some thing I want to say to all you guys out there," I said, talking to the audience. "Make sure you know an opportunity when you see it. Whether it`s working for an established publication like the New York Herald Examiner or a pretentious up-start `zine like Scorch, don`t be too proud to start at the bottom."

The exasperated host who`s show I`d usurped asked me if there was anything else I wanted to say before security booted me off-air.

"Yeah," I smiled, remembering Roxie. "Meat kills! Woo-hoo!"

* * *

Returning home, with a even more bruised and battered Salem, I found I had a appointment to see the editor at Scorch magazine - at once! I guess the publishers weren`t too happy with what I had said about them on TV…

Bursting into the editor`s office, I let loose before Annie had a chance to read me the riot act.

"If you called me down here to tell me I`m never going to work in this business," I snapped. "Well, I figured that out for myself. And that`s why I`m

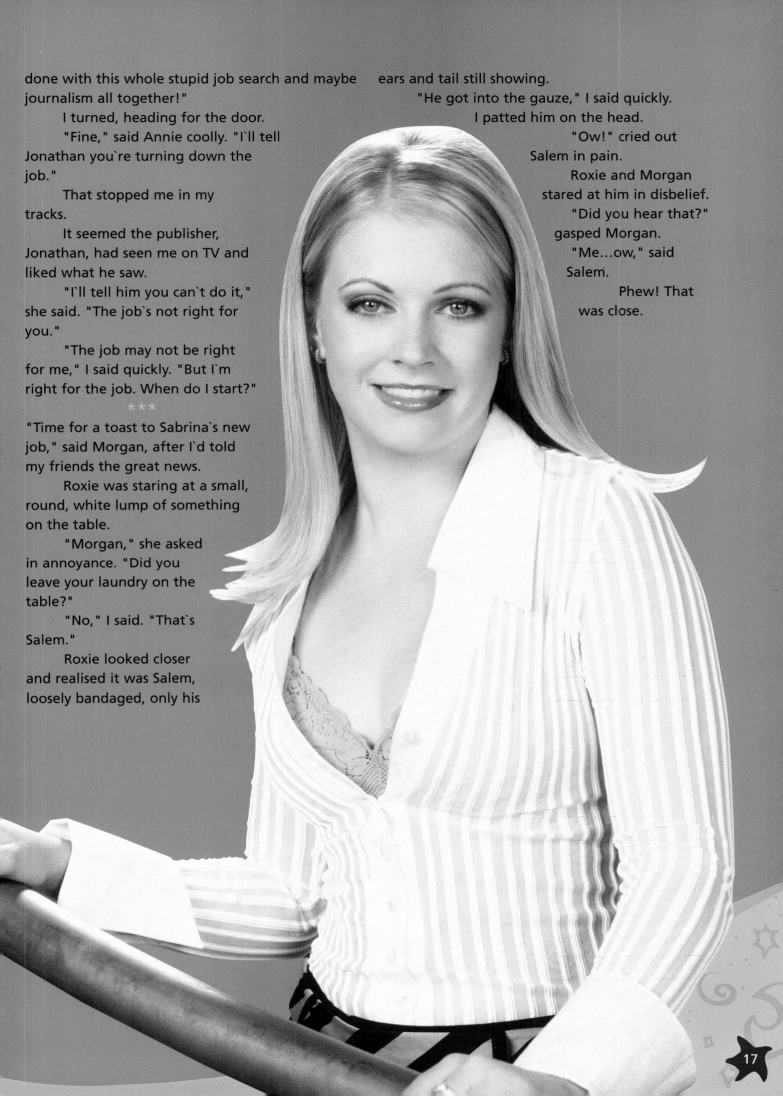

done with this whole stupid job search and maybe journalism all together!"

I turned, heading for the door.

"Fine," said Annie coolly. "I`ll tell Jonathan you`re turning down the job."

That stopped me in my tracks.

It seemed the publisher, Jonathan, had seen me on TV and liked what he saw.

"I`ll tell him you can`t do it," she said. "The job`s not right for you."

"The job may not be right for me," I said quickly. "But I`m right for the job. When do I start?"

* * *

"Time for a toast to Sabrina`s new job," said Morgan, after I`d told my friends the great news.

Roxie was staring at a small, round, white lump of something on the table.

"Morgan," she asked in annoyance. "Did you leave your laundry on the table?"

"No," I said. "That`s Salem."

Roxie looked closer and realised it was Salem, loosely bandaged, only his ears and tail still showing.

"He got into the gauze," I said quickly.

I patted him on the head.

"Ow!" cried out Salem in pain.

Roxie and Morgan stared at him in disbelief.

"Did you hear that?" gasped Morgan.

"Me...ow," said Salem.

Phew! That was close.

On The Road!

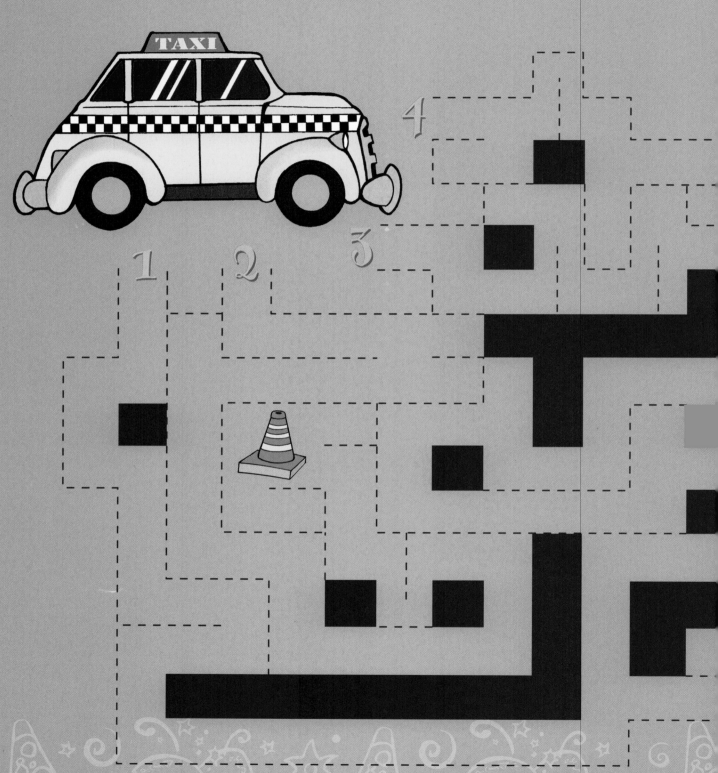

Help! Sabrina, Morgan and Roxie are late for their appointment to interview Course of Nature. Can you help them find the correct route to get them to their destination, without running into any road cones?

Answer: The correct route is entrance 3!

What's

Hi gang! Harvey here! Well, Sabrina has certainly had some changes in her life recently, what with a new job, a surly new boss and a new boyfriend (although I'd rather not comment on him). Can you place the words listed below associated with Sabrina into the grid? I've added a few letters to start you off!

3 Letters
MTV

4 Letters
COLE
JOSH

5 Letters
ANNIE
HILDA
ROXIE
SALEM
ZELDA

6 Letters
HARVEY
MORGAN

7 Letters
SABRINA

8 Letters
JONATHAN
REPORTER

9 Letters
MR FLEMING
NEWSPAPER

11 Letters
BOSTON GLOBE

14 Letters
COURSE OF NATURE
SCORCH MAGAZINE

21 Letters
NEW YORK HERALD
EXAMINER

In A Name?

Witch Way Out

Original story written by Adam Hamburger & David Hamburger

Yup, life was definitely on the up for me.

But with Aunt Zelda and Aunt Hilda no longer around, Roxie and Morgan suddenly started fussing over me as if they were my aunts.

They worried that I was working far too much at Scorch magazine, they worried I wasn`t eating properly, that I wasn`t dressing sensibly for the freezing weather...they were driving me nuts.

"Guys, I appreciate your concern," I told them, before hurrying off to work. "But I`m a grown-up. I can take care of myself."

I admit I might have been overdoing work a bit, but I was desperate to make a good impression.

Which is why I was working late at the night in the magazine offices. I was the only one there, and, man, was I bushed. Everything ached and my eyes were bleary from looking at the computer screen.

"Ohh. My neck is stiffer than," I read what was on the screen. "My writing." I`d have forced my head to confirm my thought, but it hurt too much.

Sometimes you need more than a thesaurus.

"I`ve been working `round the clock," I chanted, pointing my finger. "Help me cure my writer`s block."

PING! Next thing I knew, I was sitting in a chair that was giving me a full body massage.

"Hmm. Not what I was going for," I chuckled, enjoying the chair vibrating all my aches out of me.

"But this is nice, too."

It was then that I noticed an attractive young man standing outside the publisher`s office, staring at me! Had he seen me do a magic spell?! Gulp!

"How long have you been standing there?" I gasped, leaping up from the chair.

"Long enough to know that you are…" Uh, oh. "Are a beautiful woman."

Swoon. It turned out that his name was Victor, he owned a record label and an art gallery…and he invited me out to an opening that very night! Woo Hoo!

***

Rushing home to get ready, I found Harvey waiting there. We weren`t dating anymore, but we were just like best, best friends. Which was nice.

Anyway, while putting on my make-up, I thought saw crow`s foot around my eye from lack of sleep. I pointed to it to show Harvey and Salem, and the next thing I knew I had a real crow there.

"Why'd that happen?" Harvey wondered.

"Who knows," I scowled.

"Ever since you`ve been on this "I`m a grown-up" kick, explained Salem, "You`ve hardly been using your magic. It`s pent-up, and it`s gotta come out."

To heck with it. Who needed magic? I had been doing fine without it.

So I got a Tupperware container from the kitchen and milked all my magic out of my pointing finger and into it. No more magic for me.

Which was a pity in a way, because I would have loved to have made Roxie and Morgan disappear a few moments later. I told them about meeting Victor and the gallery opening and they thought I was inviting them to come along. Sometimes they can be so dense. Or did they just think I couldn't possibly have a date. Wait a minute…

***

Anyway, they decided we needed a `safe word`, in case either of them got cornered by a geek

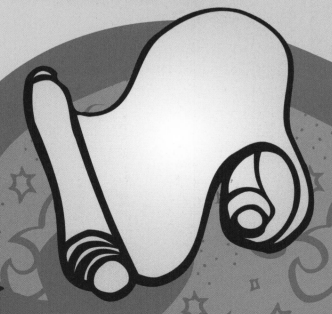

at the party and needed rescuing. We settled on `kazoo` - a word that definitely wouldn`t come up in normal conversation.

I have to admit the art in the gallery wasn`t exactly my thing…there was one sculpture that was nothing more than a twisted metal coil with an orange at the bottom of it.

However, just being with Victor made up for it. He was Prince Charming himself. And when he saw how bored I was, he invited me to the after-party at his house. That was more like it!

Of course, Roxie and Morgan weren`t too pleased about that.

"You`re going alone to a party at this guy`s house?" spluttered Roxie. "You don`t even know him."

"You need someone to come along and watch your back," agreed Morgan. "It`s called the buddy system."

I had had just about enough of their constant meddling.

"I don`t need a buddy," I snapped. "And I don`t need a chaperone. And I don`t need you guys being just like my aunts. I`m an adult. I can look out for myself."

I was sorry to hurt their feelings, , but hey, it needed to be said.

"On second thoughts, she can just buy herself a CD." This was heaven! And apparently, people work in heaven because an Asian businessman in a tuxedo entered the ballroom from a large steel door that seemed to be hidden behind a huge tapestry. He walked over to us as we danced.

"I must congratulate you," he said to Victor. "It is the rarest collection I`ve seen yet."

Victor excused himself to me, and went off to talk business.

Now you know how curiosity got the better of the cat? Well, Salem must really be rubbing off on me. I just had to see what was behind that steel door.

I tried opening it with magic, then remembered I didn`t have any. However, the code pad on the door did have redial. Hello!

The door swung open. Hurrying down a staircase, I found myself in a dimly-lit dungeon, filled with

***

The after-party was spectacular! Victor was holding it in his enormous ballroom. Loads of people were there, and he even had the Goo Goo Girls rocking out.

"Man, Morgan loves the Goo Goo Girls," I said to Victor. "Maybe I should call her?" But before I could reach for my phone, he took me in his arms and start to slow dance.

"You," he purred, looking into my eyes. "Are everything I`ve been looking for…"

cages. Each cage had a plaque, naming its contents.

The first cage, to my freaking-out horror, was filled with water and contained a beautiful real-life mermaid! The second, a wild, hairy Sasquatch.

The third cage was empty. But the plaque read, `Witch`!

"Kazoo," I groaned. I was in big trouble!

* * *

At my house, even though I had forbidden him to do so, Salem had succeeded in opening the Tupperware container to get at my magic. After all this time, I really should have known better than to trust him.

Holding a drop of magic on his paw, he read from a spell book.

"Make me human, make me whole, I`m sick of eating from a bowl."

PING! When the green smoke cleared, Salem was still a cat. But one of his paws was a human foot!

"Ohhh," he groaned. "Now the litter sand is going to get stuck between my toes!"

* * *

I stood in the Dungeon of Horrors and stared at the cage in growing disbelief. "He wants to…cage me?" I gasped.

"Oh boy, we`ve got a bright one," said a voice close by, in a lilting Irish brogue. I looked across the next cage, inside which was a tiny man in funny dress. The plaque read, `Leprechaun`.

"Are you a real leprechaun?" I asked stupidly.

"Heck, no," chuckled the leprechaun. "I`m just a short Irish guy!"

This was terrible. When Victor said he was a collector, I had no idea…

LEPRECHAUN

"I`m going to free all of you, I promise," I said, dashing back up the stairs. "But first I have to deal with this sicko!"

The `sicko` in question, of course, being Victor. After I had returned to the ballroom, I asked him to go find me some food. Lots of food. Preferably cooked for a really, really long time.

After he left, I pulled out my cell phone and called home. I needed help - fast!

Trouble was, Morgan was still mad at me.

"Well, if it isn`t Susie-Snooty society snob," she said, when she answered the phone.

Ouch. I suppose I deserved that.

"Listen," I said urgently. "This is important. Tell Harvey to come to Victor`s party with the Tupperware. Victor is…"

At that moment, Victor reappeared.

"…extremely handsome…" I said, covering myself. And then hissed quickly into the phone. "And lives in a big house on Post Road with a fountain full of peeing angels."

"Who is that?" Victor asked, puzzled.

"Kazoo! Kazoo!" I shouted into the phone, before hanging up. "Just saying hi to my cat."

"Weird name for a cat," frowned Victor.

I told Victor I really had to go, but he grabbed my arm and dragged me towards his hidden dungeons. No more Mr. Nice Guy!

"I`ve searched everywhere for a witch," he growled. "You think I`m going to let you go that easily?"

"I`m not a witch!" I spluttered weakly.

But it seems he had seen me make the massage chair magically appear, after all.

"Victor, get real" I argued. "If I don`t come home, my friends will be here in no time to save me."

Victor laughed cruelly. "You mean those two girls you ditched at the gallery? It hardly looked like they were your friends." Double Ouch.

***

At my house, Harvey realised that I was in trouble. He grabbed the Tupperware container from the kitchen, where Salem sat licking his human foot.

"Mmm, I`d forgotten how good this feels," he purred.

"Do something about that foot," said Harvey, giving him some magic. "It`s disgusting."

While my friends dashed to my rescue, Salem slapped the magic on his foot. "Magic spell gone kaput," he said. "Help me fix this ugly foot."

PING! An elegant slipper appeared on the foot.

"That`s better," said Salem.

* * *

Victor had locked me in a cage next to the Sasquatch, and without my magic, I couldn`t escape.

He was crowing to me about how much I`d fetch at auction, when there came a pounding on the front door.

"That must be my pizza," he said, climbing up the staircase. "Excuse me, won`t you?"

"This is all my fault," I groaned, slumping to the floor of the cage. "My friends warned me. They wanted to protect me and all I did was treat them like dirt."

"Yeah," agreed the leprechaun. "Friends are important."

Upstairs, Victor discovered it wasn`t the pizza delivery - it was Harvey, Roxie and Morgan.

When they demanded to know where I was, Victor allowed them inside to see that everyone was gone. They were about to leave when they heard loud roaring coming from the basement.

That would have been Sasquatch reacting to me hitting him on the head with the handle of a witch`s broom Victor had placed in my cage. I knew it wasn`t nice, but desperate times call for desperate measures.

Victor tried to quickly hustle my friends out of the house.

Morgan kept him occupied, giving Roxie and Harvey the chance to find the steel door. They split up to maximise their manpower. Luckily, my magic was drawn to me and led Harvey right to the hidden door. When he was sure Morgan and Roxie couldn't see what he was doing, he opened the Tupperware and spilled out my magic goo.

It poured through the lock and the door sprang open. Harvey followed the magic puddle into the dungeons.

"Sabrina!" he cried, watching the magic

jump through the bars of the cage and down my throat. "Are you okay?"

Well, apart from the rotten taste, I was fine. I could feel the magic spreading through me again! I pointed to myself and I was free.

Suddenly, Victor appeared, stalking down the stairs towards us.

"Going somewhere?" he hissed, menacingly.

"Sabrina," Harvey gulped nervously. "I know you're all grown up and don't want to use your magic - - "

"Yeah, whatever," I said. I pointed my finger at Victor and he was inside the Sasquatch's cage, and not feeling much love from the big guy. Serves him right!

As I sent all the mythical creatures back to their homes, I told Harvey, "There are two things I`m very lucky to have: my magic and my friends." Luckily, my friends felt the same way about me and accepted my apology for the way I`d behaved.

* * *

A few days later, after I`d fixed Salem`s feet so they all matched again, I was at home, suffering a nasty cold.

"I`ll make chicken soup," said Roxie.

"I`ll get the thermometer," said Morgan.

"Wait," commanded Roxie. "We`re doing it again!"

Morgan agreed. "Yep, we`re being her aunts."

"Be them!" I pleaded.

But no, they went shopping instead.

"I`m feeling lousy here!" I shouted after them. "Auntie Morgan! Auntie Roxie! Anti-histamine!"

WITCH

It's A Myth!

Geez, that Victor was a one scary guy! If you ask me, HE'S the one that belongs in a zoo. Ha! Anyway, it's a good thing he never came over to our house when Sabrina used to invite some of her favourite mythological creatures to visit.

Fairies

Fairies, or faeries as they are sometimes known, bestow gifts upon unborn children, such as beauty, kindness and wealth. They usually can only be seen clearly by animals, except when they use their powers (known as `glamour`) to let a human see them. They can also be seen, if you look hard enough, at the bottom of the garden during a full moon on Midsummer`s Eve, when you`ll witness fairy dances and celebrations!

Gnome

Gnomes are a race of ugly, misshapen, dwarf-like creatures who live under the earth, guarding priceless treasures. They rarely appear above ground, as even one ray of sunlight will turn them to stone. (Why do you think you see some many garden gnomes around?!) Some people suspect that during daylight hours they spend time disguised as a toad!

Gremlin

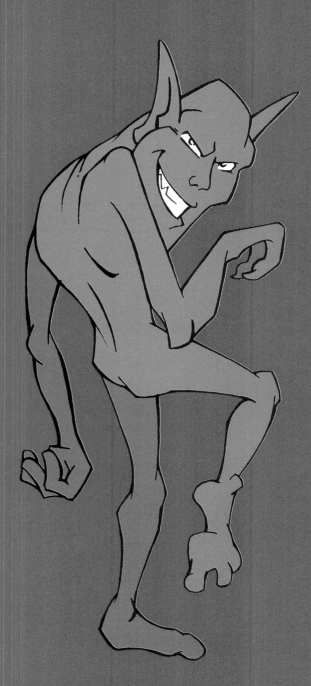

Oooh! I can`t stand these pests! They`re mischievous little spirits of tools and machinery, and are personally responsible for all the small accidents people suffer when working with tools, such as hitting your thumb with a hammer when driving in a nail! OUCH!

They hold down toaster levers so your bread burns, blunt all sharp objects such as knives, saws and chisels, and play with the hot and cold water when you`re taking a shower! EEEK! Anything that goes wrong, blame a gremlin! (or a cat named Salem, if you've got one)

Mermaid

You might be surprised to learn that mermaids are not as nice as you might think (but they still don't deserve to be in Victor's "collection")! A mermaid (sometimes called a Sea Witch) is a marine creature with the head and upper body of a beautiful maiden, and the lower body of a fish. They can be found in seas and lakes, luring unsuspecting sailors to their doom by their beautiful music and singing voices! (That let`s out Zelda!)

Dragon

Dragons are huge, fire-breathing, lizard-like creatures, with long fangs, twin horns of varying length, and large, bat-like wings that give them the capability of flight over long distances. Dragons are either covered in scales, or have tough, leathery skin The most common colours are black, green, red or gold. Magical in nature, dragons are solitary animals, who prefer to stay away from human contact. (except when they're brides-to-be on a rampage - but I'm getting ahead of things)

Unicorn

Sabrina's favourite mythical creature! Unicorns have the body of a pure white horse, a spiralling horn in the centre of its forehead, and deep blue eyes. The horn possesses special healing abilities, and dust from the horn protects against poisons and many diseases.

Giants

Primitive creatures of enormous size, giants have existed long before either humans or gods, and are the hated enemies of both! When the gods first appeared there was a cataclysmic battle between the two which the giants eventually lost. Giants can either be very dim and greedy, or else they can be kind and gentle and the friends of little children.

The Loch Ness Monster

The world`s most famous mythical creature might still exist today! Living in the deep, gloomy depths of Loch Ness in the Highlands of Scotland, Nessie, as it is fondly known, is 12-15 metres in length, has a long, extended neck, and is believed to be female. Sightings date back to 565 AD, when the Irish Saint Columba claimed he saw Nessie while attending the burial of a man bitten to death by a sea monster!

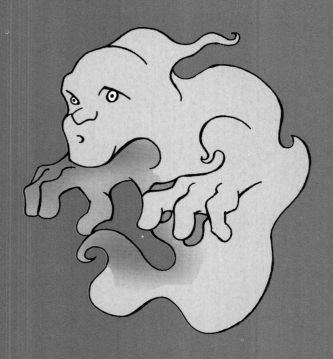

Will-O'-The-Wisp

Usually a soft, bluish light, but also reddish or greenish in colour, these are naughty imps and pixies who lead their victims into danger in swamps and heaths, many times causing them to drown. They`re also known as Jack O` Lantern, Spunkie and Fox Fire. The classical name for them is Ignus Fatuus (`Fool`s Fire`).

The Abominable Snowman

Existing in the mountains of the Himalayas since at least the 4th Century BC, the Yeti (literally meaning `magical creature`) is called a `rakshasa` by the people of Napal, which is Sanskrit for `demon`! It has reddish hair, smells terrible and is extremely strong. It roars like a lion and is very fond of alcoholic drinks! (wonder how they found out about that?)

Friends Forever!

Well, in trying to please all my friends, I almost lost them! If you`d like to seal a friendship with someone you like, what better than to make them this beautiful Friendship Bracelet as a special gift?

You will need:

6 stranded colour thread, two of each colour, 100cm long (from craft shop). We have used pink, purple and yellow thread, but you can choose any colour you like!
Scissors
Sticky tape (Or whatever you call Sellotape these days)
Piece of cardboard

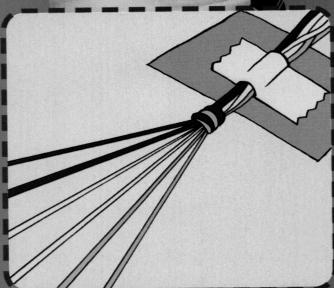

1 Tie all six strands of thread together into a knot roughly 10cm from the top of the thread. Using the sticky tape, fasten the threads onto the cardboard, close to the knot.

2 Take the thread on the far left (in this case, a purple thread) and take over the purple thread next to it, then back under the thread, through the loop and over itself. Carefully pull the thread to make a knot.

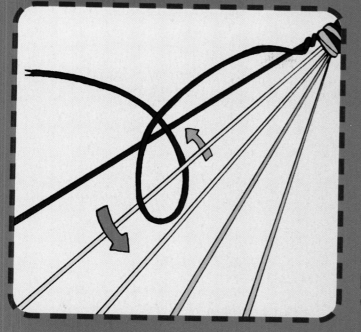

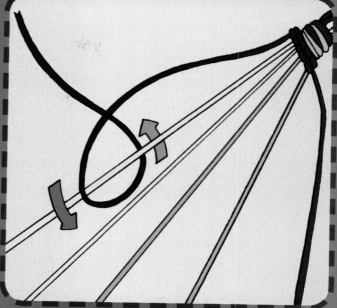

3 Repeat instruction 2. Using the same thread, make two knots on the yellow thread. Knot the rest of the yellow and pink threads with the purple thread until you have reached the end of the first row.

4 Return to the new thread on the far left, which in this case is another purple thread, and repeat steps 2 and 3 until you`ve made another row. The new thread on the far left is now a yellow thread. Again, knot this in the same way.

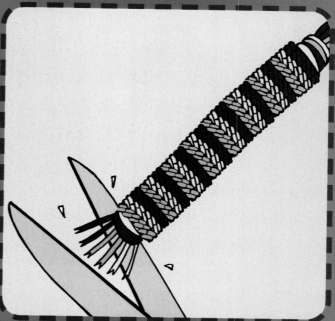

5 Keep on knotting each new far left thread over the other threads. This will create stripes of the three different colours. Continue this until the bracelet is the right length to fit around your wrist.

6 Tie a knot into the threads at the end of the braid. Plait the loose threads at both ends of the bracelet for 6cm and secure with knots. Trim any uneven threads with scissors. (Ask a grown-up to help!)

Present Perfect

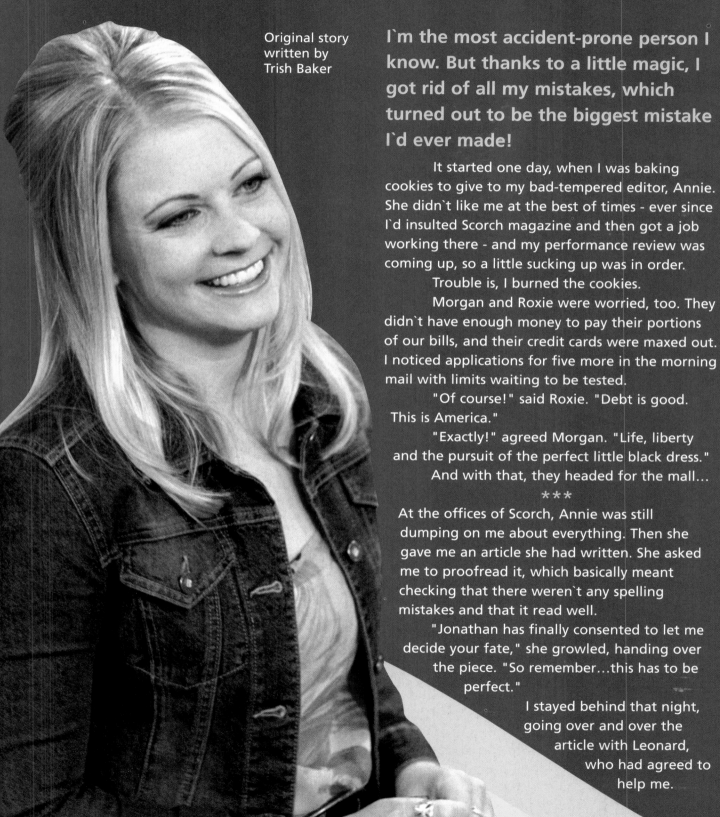

Original story written by Trish Baker

I`m the most accident-prone person I know. But thanks to a little magic, I got rid of all my mistakes, which turned out to be the biggest mistake I`d ever made!

It started one day, when I was baking cookies to give to my bad-tempered editor, Annie. She didn`t like me at the best of times - ever since I`d insulted Scorch magazine and then got a job working there - and my performance review was coming up, so a little sucking up was in order.

Trouble is, I burned the cookies.

Morgan and Roxie were worried, too. They didn`t have enough money to pay their portions of our bills, and their credit cards were maxed out. I noticed applications for five more in the morning mail with limits waiting to be tested.

"Of course!" said Roxie. "Debt is good. This is America."

"Exactly!" agreed Morgan. "Life, liberty and the pursuit of the perfect little black dress."

And with that, they headed for the mall...

***

At the offices of Scorch, Annie was still dumping on me about everything. Then she gave me an article she had written. She asked me to proofread it, which basically meant checking that there weren`t any spelling mistakes and that it read well.

"Jonathan has finally consented to let me decide your fate," she growled, handing over the piece. "So remember...this has to be perfect."

I stayed behind that night, going over and over the article with Leonard, who had agreed to help me.

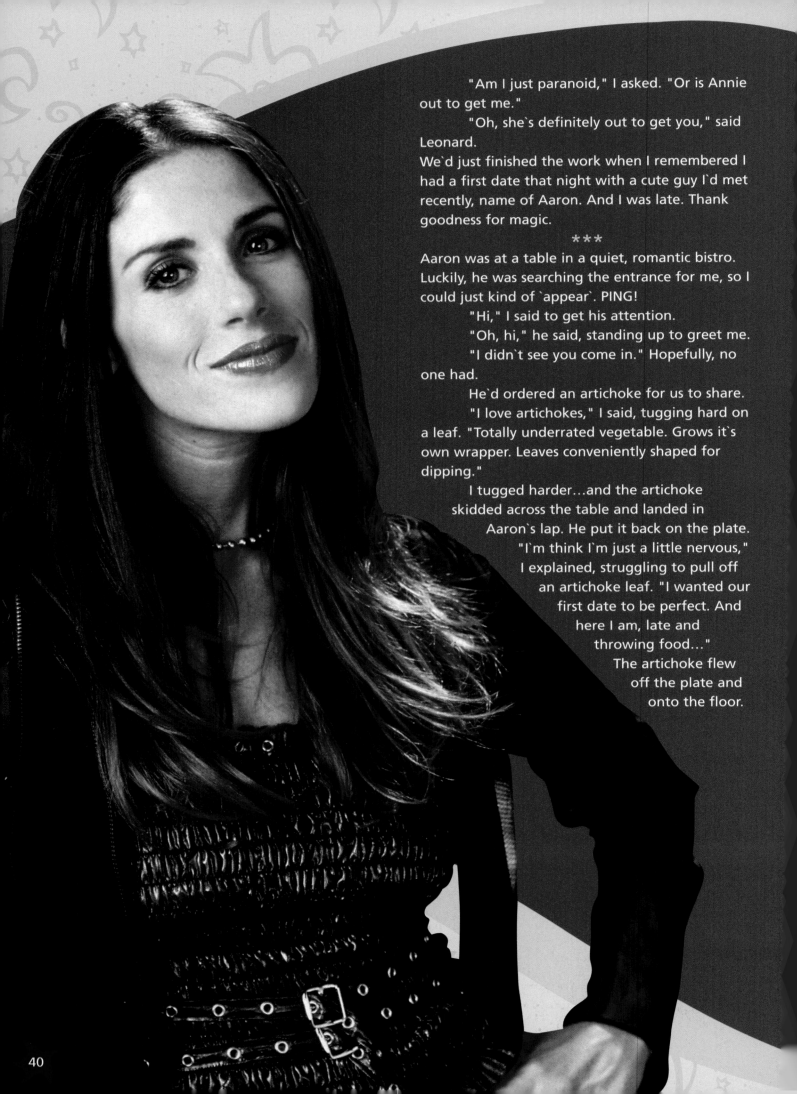

"Am I just paranoid," I asked. "Or is Annie out to get me."

"Oh, she`s definitely out to get you," said Leonard.

We`d just finished the work when I remembered I had a first date that night with a cute guy I`d met recently, name of Aaron. And I was late. Thank goodness for magic.

***

Aaron was at a table in a quiet, romantic bistro. Luckily, he was searching the entrance for me, so I could just kind of `appear`. PING!

"Hi," I said to get his attention.

"Oh, hi," he said, standing up to greet me.

"I didn`t see you come in." Hopefully, no one had.

He`d ordered an artichoke for us to share.

"I love artichokes," I said, tugging hard on a leaf. "Totally underrated vegetable. Grows it`s own wrapper. Leaves conveniently shaped for dipping."

I tugged harder...and the artichoke skidded across the table and landed in Aaron`s lap. He put it back on the plate.

"I`m think I`m just a little nervous," I explained, struggling to pull off an artichoke leaf. "I wanted our first date to be perfect. And here I am, late and throwing food..."

The artichoke flew off the plate and onto the floor.

"...all over the restaurant." I then tried to pull the leaf off with my teeth, and accidentally flipped it onto Aaron`s nose.

"So," he said, grinning, removing the leaf. "Seen any good movies?"

I sank into my chair, totally mortified.

* * *

It didn`t get much better when he took me home. We had a little directional problem manoeuvring for a good night kiss and I would up biting his nose!

"That was officially the worst date of my entire life," I groaned, finding Roxie and Morgan in the living room. "There is no way he`s ever going to want to go out with me again."

My roommates sympathized. They offered to buy me something to cheer me up. Seems with those new credit cards they now had a hundred thousand dollar credit limit.

I trudged upstairs and, being tired and upset that because of my mistakes I`d probably never see Aaron again, I stupidly accepted help from Salem. He said that if a witch`s appendix is removed, she`ll be mistake free.

Perfect. I cast a spell, and an Other Realm surgeon appeared in my room. He pointed a finger and - PING! - one removed appendix. And not a scar to be seen.

No more mistakes from me. Woo Hoo! But being perfect brought its own troubles.

After eight hours sleep in a perfectly made bed, I was ready to start a perfect day. Unfortunately, not everyone was as flawless as I`d become. Guess I`d just have to show them how things should be done.

First, I showed Roxie and Morgan how to use their credit cards more profitably. Then at work, I fixed the printer for Cole and picked the perfect pictures for James (the ones he`d chosen were all wrong!).

Then, proving this to be the perfect beginning to my new perfect life, Aaron came by to take me to lunch. The restaurant was nice, but less than perfect.

"I`m pretty sure my side of the table cloth is hanging lower than yours," I said. "And there`s a stain." I yanked at the table cloth, out from under the place settings with perfect grace so that nothing moved.

"And this place has got four stars," I groaned.

I settled in for a perfect lunch, but was distracted by a man eating lobster at the next table. Or trying to. He was doing it all wrong. Not in my perfect world, buddy!

"Excuse me," I said to a open-mouthed Aaron, and hurried over to the man`s table.

I grabbed the lobster from the startled guy`s hands. "If I may...first you pluck off the claws, like so. Then you pinch here and here so you access the tail..." The lobster split open perfectly.

Aaron must have been impressed with me, because all he could do was stare at me as I returned to the table.

"Wow. Between you and I," he said. "I had no idea you were such a...stickler."

"Well, I said, correcting him." Between you and me, I`m not."

"What do you say we get the cheque?" he suggested, rather abruptly. What was his problem, I wondered?

* * *

Time to get back to work, where I found a fuming Annie. Without her knowledge, I had `improved` a few things in the upcoming magazine, including her article.

"Spellman, what is this?! You`ve changed the layout, you altered the titles...you re-wrote

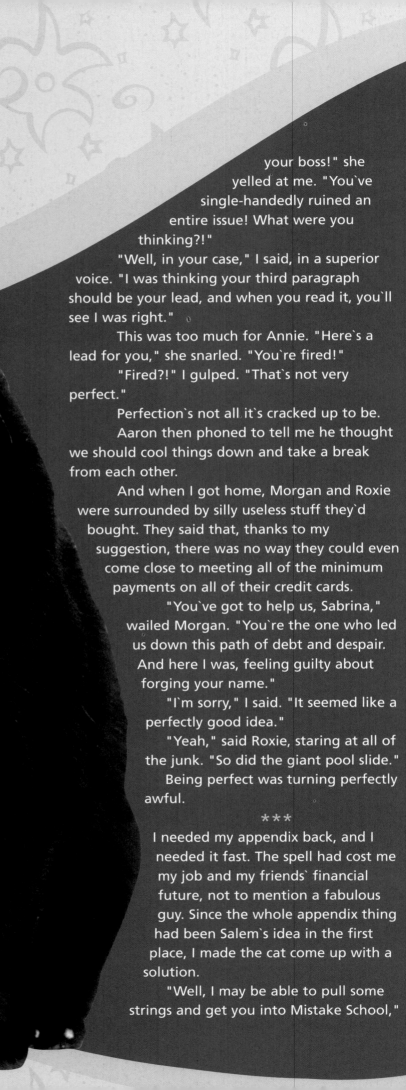

your boss!" she yelled at me. "You`ve single-handedly ruined an entire issue! What were you thinking?!"

"Well, in your case," I said, in a superior voice. "I was thinking your third paragraph should be your lead, and when you read it, you`ll see I was right."

This was too much for Annie. "Here`s a lead for you," she snarled. "You`re fired!"

"Fired?!" I gulped. "That`s not very perfect."

Perfection`s not all it`s cracked up to be.

Aaron then phoned to tell me he thought we should cool things down and take a break from each other.

And when I got home, Morgan and Roxie were surrounded by silly useless stuff they`d bought. They said that, thanks to my suggestion, there was no way they could even come close to meeting all of the minimum payments on all of their credit cards.

"You`ve got to help us, Sabrina," wailed Morgan. "You`re the one who led us down this path of debt and despair. And here I was, feeling guilty about forging your name."

"I`m sorry," I said. "It seemed like a perfectly good idea."

"Yeah," said Roxie, staring at all of the junk. "So did the giant pool slide."

Being perfect was turning perfectly awful.

***

I needed my appendix back, and I needed it fast. The spell had cost me my job and my friends` financial future, not to mention a fabulous guy. Since the whole appendix thing had been Salem`s idea in the first place, I made the cat come up with a solution.

"Well, I may be able to pull some strings and get you into Mistake School,"

he offered. Seems it was an Other Realm school for people having trouble with mistakes.

Sounded good to me! Forget his `strings`, I`ve got PING! I pointed a finger at myself and the next moment I was sitting in a college classroom with lots of other students who had made mistakes, including a fat Roman Emperor holding a violin, a guy with a drill in his head...and General Custer himself.

They were being lectured to by a warlock instructor at the front of the class.

"...Okay, people we`ve been over this before. The comb-over, always a mistake. Clogs on men? Big mistake!"

I raised my hand, interrupting him.

"Excuse me. I`m Sabrina Spellman and I`ve misplaced my appendix. Consequently, I`ve lost my job and my boyfriend. So I really just need to learn how to make mistakes again and I`ll be on my way."

The instructor stared at me.

"Lost your boyfriend and your job? Sounds like you already

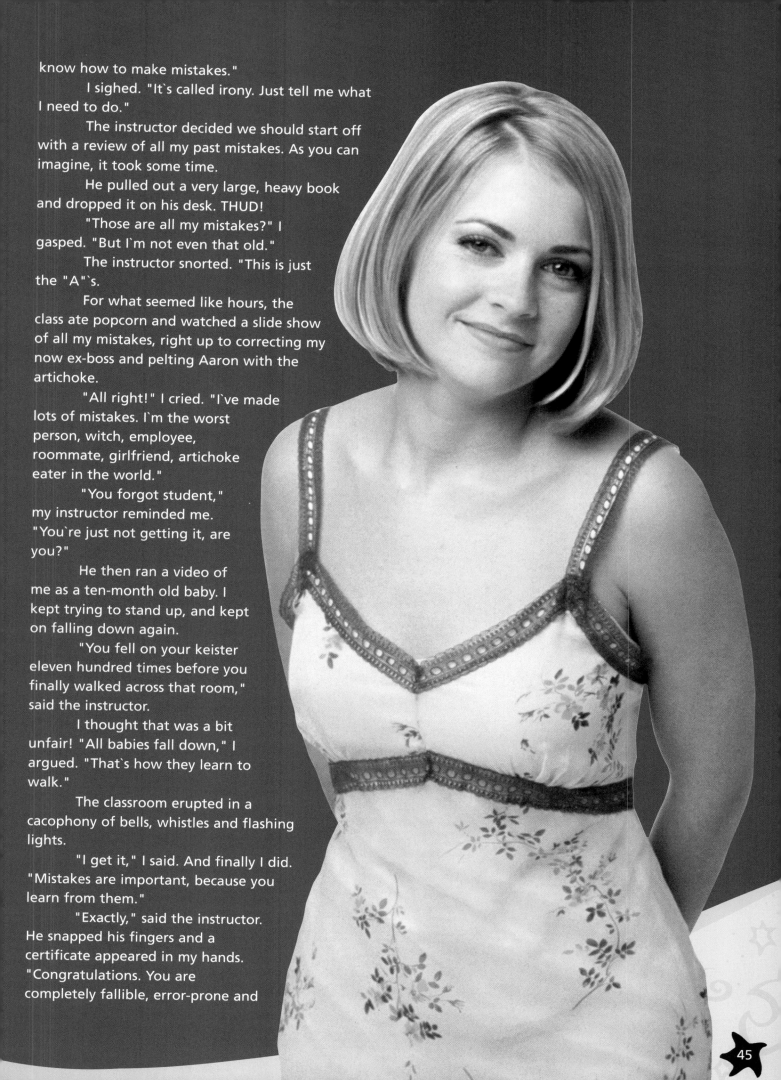

know how to make mistakes."

I sighed. "It`s called irony. Just tell me what I need to do."

The instructor decided we should start off with a review of all my past mistakes. As you can imagine, it took some time.

He pulled out a very large, heavy book and dropped it on his desk. THUD!

"Those are all my mistakes?" I gasped. "But I`m not even that old."

The instructor snorted. "This is just the "A"`s.

For what seemed like hours, the class ate popcorn and watched a slide show of all my mistakes, right up to correcting my now ex-boss and pelting Aaron with the artichoke.

"All right!" I cried. "I`ve made lots of mistakes. I`m the worst person, witch, employee, roommate, girlfriend, artichoke eater in the world."

"You forgot student," my instructor reminded me. "You`re just not getting it, are you?"

He then ran a video of me as a ten-month old baby. I kept trying to stand up, and kept on falling down again.

"You fell on your keister eleven hundred times before you finally walked across that room," said the instructor.

I thought that was a bit unfair! "All babies fall down," I argued. "That`s how they learn to walk."

The classroom erupted in a cacophony of bells, whistles and flashing lights.

"I get it," I said. And finally I did. "Mistakes are important, because you learn from them."

"Exactly," said the instructor. He snapped his fingers and a certificate appeared in my hands. "Congratulations. You are completely fallible, error-prone and

will definitely make many mistakes during your lifetime."
I couldn`t wait to get started and proved it when I walked into the door as I left the classroom. Ouch.

* * *

Returning home, I fixed my first mistake, giving money advice to my friends. I cut up all our credit cards. No more getting into debt.

Now it was time to apologise to Annie. Surprisingly, she said she`d give me a second chance. I told her I had a great idea for an article but she shot me down in flames.

"Don`t waste my time," she snapped. The last thing I need to do is slog my way through another tedious Spellman hack piece."

"Oh, okay," I said, glad to have a job again Then I realised I was making a big mistake.

"No, not okay," I argued. "Not okay, at all! I admit I might make the occasional mistake. But the biggest mistake I made here was not standing up to you months ago. I`m not a hack. I`m a really good writer, and I bust my butt day in and day out for you. And there`s no reason why I should ever have to be treated like this."

Annie was shocked, to say the least.
"You`re going to just walk out of here?" she screamed, as I left the office. "You`re making a huge mistake."

"I don`t think so," I said. "But if I am, I`ll learn."

* * *

Boy, that felt good. I think. Oh, well. I`d find another job. Eventually. Two down, and one to go. Luckily, I didn`t have to go far to look to make amends with Aaron. I stormed out of the office right into him. And he was, well, perfect.

"I realised you were just trying to make everything…perfect," he told me. "And that`s sweet and flattering, but, Sabrina, I love it when you wrestle vegetables and show up late - -

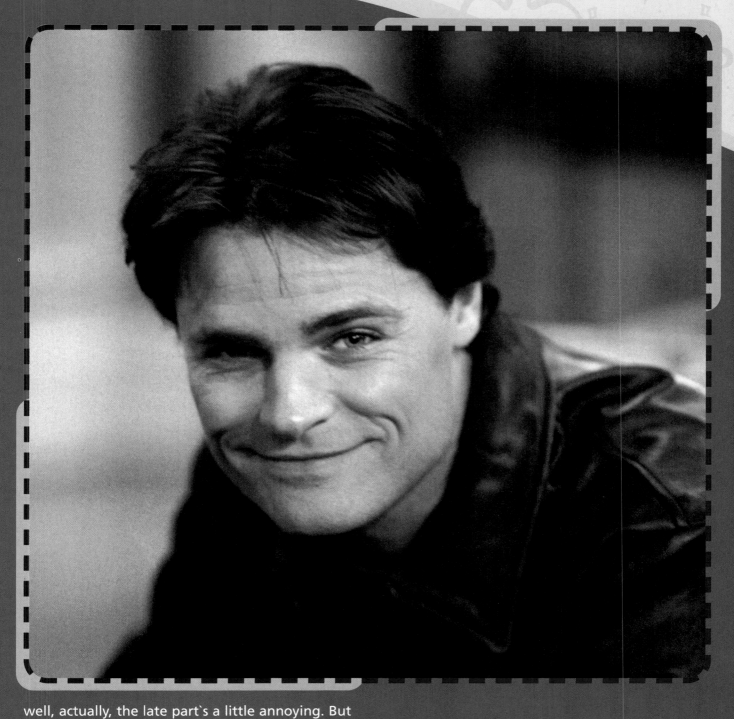

well, actually, the late part`s a little annoying. But
the point is, I don`t want someone who`s perfect."

I grinned. "Then it`s your lucky day."

If any moment called for a kiss! But we still
couldn`t seem to get it right. First we leaned
one way, then the other, and then we
bumped noses. But the kiss was
definitely worth the trouble.

"Absolutely
perfect," said Aaron.

Blunder Wall

Boy, being perfect isn`t all it`s cracked up to be. I`ll think I`ll remain good ol`, accident-prone Sabrina from now on! As you`ll notice, I`ve already made some mistakes in this puzzle!

Can you find a word in the wall to match each of the 21 clues? There are four answers left over which aren`t in the wall. Can you name them? Which words in the wall are listed twice? And of these, which is the odd one out?

Questions

1. Sabrina`s ex-boyfriend?
2. The editor of Scorch magazine?
3. Sabrina turned down a job at the Boston .....?
4. What Salem used to be and Sabrina`s dad still is?
5. Sabrina`s surname is ....?
6. In New York, Salem was beaten up by a giant ...?
7. The Witches' Council lives in the Other .....?
8. Sabrina`s mother`s name is .....?
9. Sabrina`s favourite cat!
10. A witch casts magic ......?
11. We all know Sabrina`s Aunt Zelda and Aunt .....?
12. Harvey`s favourite two-wheeled vehicle to ride?
13. If Sabrina`s mom ever seens Sabrina again, she`ll turn into a ball of ...?

14. The name of Sabrina's DJ housemate?

15. Witches traditionally stirred up spells in a magic ....?

16. Sabrina has recently graduated from ....?

17. Roxie and Morgan live with Sabrina in her Aunt's .....?

18. The name of our favourite witch's father?

19. Diana Spellman is on an archaeological dig in ....?

20. A tiny Irish magical imp?

21. The name of Sabrina's new boyfriend?

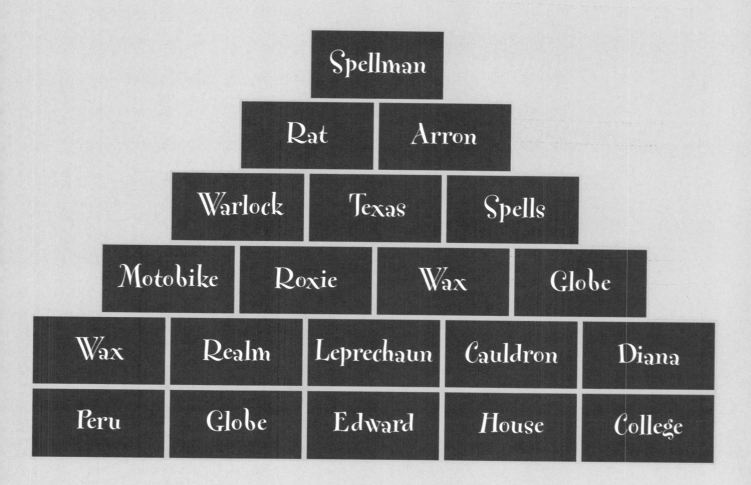

Who's That?

As you can see, I`m not Little Miss Perfect anymore! Can you recognize my friends and family under the paint splodges I`ve spilled over their photographs?

Sabrina The Teenage Witch™

It's A Joke!

Poor Sabrina tried so hard to be perfect, she forgot to have fun! So here's some of her favourite witch jokes to cheer her up!

Q. Why is a witch like a candle?
A. **They are both wick-ed!**

Q. What happened to the witch with the upsidedown nose?
A. **Every time she sneezed, she blew her hat off!**

Q. What do you call a witch with poison ivy?
A. **An itchy witchy!**

Q. How do witches tell the time?
A. **With their witch watches!**

Q. What do witch racers ride on?
A. **Vrooomsticks!**

Juggle This!

Salem's showing off how good he is at juggling - or so he thought! Re-arrange the jumbled-up letters in the balls to spell out things you might see at a circus. Each ball has an extra letter, which will spell out a hidden circus word!

4
S N R R I T
E M S A
R G

5
A N F
Y S T T
O T E
E

6
E R T P
A E P
Z

3
I O T P
I A G
B

7
S O W
C N
R L

2
U G G L S
E C J
G R

1
G E R H
E T B
P O I T

8
D
C U E
I A A
N E

Cirque du Sabrina

Original story
written by
Suzanne Gangursky

Hey, feline fans. Salem here. I thought it`d be fun to hijack Sabrina`s annual and tell you a true tale of love, jealousy, a bad hair day and...the circus.

Unknown to Sabrina, her life was starting to unravel faster than her Cashmere sweater caught in my dew claw. She was trying to balance being there for both her friends and her boyfriend at the same time.

She had promised to go to a business dinner with Aaron and leave there in time to watch Harvey play in a hockey game. Except she had so much fun with Aaron, she never made it to the game.

"I`m cool," said Harvey, who was waiting for her when she finally returned home with Aaron, and she had grovelled apologies. "I`ve got another one tomorrow."

"Perfect," said Sabrina. "We wouldn`t miss it for the world."

Aaron pulled out two tickets from his jacket. "The world, no," he said, "But a world premiere, yes." He handed the tickets to a shocked Sabrina. "I was going to surprise you with tickets to the Boston Film Festival."

"Oh," gasped Sabrina, excitedly. "I've always wanted…." She looked guiltily at a disappointed Harvey. "How about Wednesday?"

Morgan piped up - Sabrina had promised to do her hair that day. And Roxie had made plans with Sabrina to try a new yoga class. And then Aaron reminded her that they had made plans for Wednesday, too.

"I've got everything perfectly under control," she told me, heading for her bedroom after saying kissy-kissy goodnight to Aaron. "I've just got to do a little juggling."

Well, you know how literal things are with witches. Sabrina entered her room, and FOOMP! she was blinded by a giant spotlight shining in her face. When stars had stopped exploding in the back of her eyes, she found her bedroom had turned into the centre ring of a circus!
She was dressed in a sparkly aerialist's outfit, and a French Ringmaster was juggling four red balls. Only Sabrina's real life could be more bizarre than her dreams.

"Mind telling me why you're here and why I'm dressed like a Russian figure skater?" she demanded.

The Ringmaster explained that he pitched his tent wherever and whenever he found a witch who's life was seriously out of balance.

The Ringmaster threw the four balls at Sabrina, each with one of her friends names on, and she suddenly found herself on a tightrope fifteen metres in the air. He told her that if her life was really balanced she would have no trouble crossing the tightrope while juggling the balls.

I'll give Sabrina credit for trying. Like she had any choice. She managed two steps before falling. Luckily, there was a safety net.

"Okay. Maybe my life is a bit out of balance," she admitted. "But it shouldn't be too hard to fix."
I hope not," declared the Ringmaster. Because until you make it to the far platform, Cirque du Sabrina is here to stay."

* * *

Sabrina woke up pretty grouchy the next morning.

"I can't believe I had to spend the night on the couch just because the stupid circus came to town," she complained.

"You think you've got it bad?" I growled. "Try driving around in a tiny car with fourteen French clowns."

This might have evoked more sympathy had I not been wearing a big red nose, a crunched hat and giant clown shoes on my normally dainty paws.

Sabrina still insisted that everything in her life was going great, so I pointed out that Aaron was jealous of Harvey spending so much time with her.

"No guy wants his girlfriend hanging around with her ex," I explained. "Trust me…I'm a man…turned into a cat…turned into a clown." I let out a painful groan. "Oh, kill me now."

Determined to prove me wrong, Sabrina went to see Aaron. To her surprise, he admitted he was jealous.

"Cone on," Sabrina protested. "Harvey is so fat past an ex, he's a `y`."

"Say what you want, I just don't like having him around," Aaron argued.

"Relationships are about compromise," she snapped back. "But this isn't one of those times. Harvey is my friend. I can't be with someone who wants to dictate who I see and who I don't."

And with that, Sabrina stormed out. Or she would have if she could have found the door.

Okay, solving that problem had to have put things back in balance, right? Wrong! That Ringmaster

was becoming a really big pain in the derriere.

Next thing Sabrina knew, she was back on the tightrope, holding a long pole. She was doing pretty well this time, until Aaron appeared on one end of the pole and Harvey the other. Yeah, you guessed it. She wound up falling on her keister in that safety net again.

"I do not think the jealous boyfriend is your problem," said the Ringmaster.

"Then what is?" Sabrina wondered.

"Me," said Harvey, who had fallen with Sabrina. Or was that `for` her? "I`m still in love with you, Sabrina."

Didn`t see that one comin`, didya?

***

In shock, Sabrina left her room and ran into Roxie, who, in Sabrina`s stead, had made a big mess

of Morgan's hair and was running out of ways to keep her from noticing.

"Harvey's still in love with me," Sabrina said.

Roxie's face lit up. "Sabrina, that's fantastic. This kind of gossip will keep Morgan distracted for hours."

But before anyone had a chance to discuss things further, Aaron called.

"Listen, I'm sorry about the whole Harvey thing," he told Sabrina, unaware that he'd had good cause to be jealous. "I just called Harvey and asked him to join us at the club tonight."

"You are the greatest boyfriend ever," Sabrina told him, and hung up. "I am the worst girlfriend ever."

"Sabrina," said Morgan, unaware that her hair had now changed to a lovely shade of pink. Or that Roxie was busy pulling out chunks of it. "It's not your fault Harvey's not over you. Odd, but not your fault."

Roxie enthusiastically agreed. "Good point, Morgan," she gulped, staring at the hair in growing panic. "Is anything ever really anyone's fault?"

"You know, you're absolutely right," said Sabrina, heading back up the stairs. "This isn't my problem. This is Harvey's problem. The circus should be in his room." The girls stared at her, puzzled. "As the old saying goes," said Sabrina, weakly.

***

"You say you cannot change his feelings," the Ringmaster said, when Sabrina confronted him. Way to state the obvious, Frenchy. "But what if he never had them at all?" Hmm, interesting option.

With a little sleight of hand, he reached behind Sabrina`s ear and pulled out a long silk scarf.

"The feelings that upset you today are connected to those of yesterday," he told her. The scarf was connected to a second scarf. "And those from the day before that." He pulled out a third scarf, a fourth, a fifth…

"I`m going to be here awhile, aren`t I?" sighed Sabrina.

The Ringmaster laughed. "Americans. Always in a hurry." He pulled out even more scarves. "And the day before that…"

Meanwhile, Roxie and Morgan, her hair concealed under a huge scarf, were meeting with Harvey at a diner. He vehemently denied still being in love with Sabrina, and insisted they were just good friends. But when he paid the bill, a photo of him and Sabrina fell out of his wallet.

"Do you carry all your friends` photos with you?" asked Roxie.

Harvey sighed. "Okay. It was our first Valentine`s Day. We were young and at the mall…" And proving he said one thing and felt another, he grabbed back the photo from Morgan. "Give me that!"

***

At the Cirque du Sabrina, there was a huge pile of scarves on the floor. The Ringmaster was still pulling even more scarves from her ear.

"…and the day before that, and the day

before that," he intoned. "All leading back to that day when the first spark of love was ignited."

He pulled out a last scarf. Sabrina stared at a film being screened on the scarf of the first time she and Harvey saw each other in the school corridor.

"Wow," she sighed. "Could I get that on DVD?"

"The question is," said the Ringmaster. "What shall we do with this moment."

"I`d like to keep it," groaned Sabrina. "But if this is what`s throwing my life out of balance, I can only imagine what it`s doing to Harvey."

So with the flick of a wrist, the Ringmaster made the scarf - and Harvey`s feelings for Sabrina! - disappear forever!

"Voila!" said the Ringmaster, taking a bow. "Impressive, no?"

"Uh, not really," said Sabrina. "I`m a witch, remember?"

While Sabrina was sorting out her contorted love life, I`d found a little love of my own. I`d scored a date with one of the contortionists from the circus.

"Just like you to turn my personal tragedy into a romantic opportunity," Sabrina growled when I told her.

"Yup," I purred happily. "Everybody wins."

Then the doorbell rang and it was Aaron, coming to pick up Sabrina and take her to the club.

"Harvey`s going to be there, right?" asked Sabrina.

As they left the house, I could hear Aaron muttering to himself under his breath, "I`m not jealous! I`m not jealous." Ahh, young love. What soft tissues were invented for.

The club was crowded and Sabrina couldn`t find Harvey anywhere. Then she spotted him making his way to the bar.

"I`ll be right back," she told Aaron, hurrying over to him. "Don`t go away."

The green-eyed monster flashed momentarily in Aaron`s eyes. "Why would I go away," he hissed to himself. "When Harvey`s here?!"

"Hey, Harvey," said Sabrina, greeting him warmly.

Harvey turned and looked disinterestedly at her. "Oh, hi Spellman." He turned back to the bartender, ignoring her.

Sabrina frowned. "I just wanted to do a little check. See how you`re feeling about us."

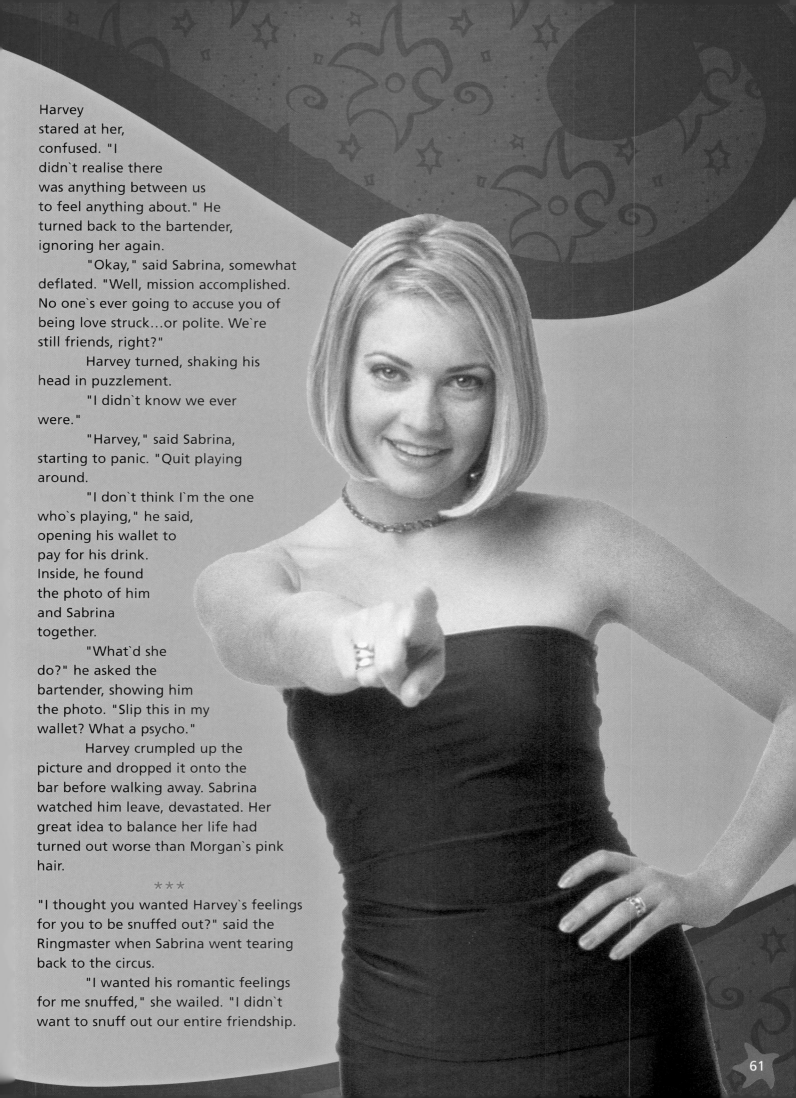

Harvey stared at her, confused. "I didn`t realise there was anything between us to feel anything about." He turned back to the bartender, ignoring her again.

"Okay," said Sabrina, somewhat deflated. "Well, mission accomplished. No one`s ever going to accuse you of being love struck...or polite. We`re still friends, right?"

Harvey turned, shaking his head in puzzlement.

"I didn`t know we ever were."

"Harvey," said Sabrina, starting to panic. "Quit playing around.

"I don`t think I`m the one who`s playing," he said, opening his wallet to pay for his drink. Inside, he found the photo of him and Sabrina together.

"What`d she do?" he asked the bartender, showing him the photo. "Slip this in my wallet? What a psycho."

Harvey crumpled up the picture and dropped it onto the bar before walking away. Sabrina watched him leave, devastated. Her great idea to balance her life had turned out worse than Morgan`s pink hair.

* * *

"I thought you wanted Harvey`s feelings for you to be snuffed out?" said the Ringmaster when Sabrina went tearing back to the circus.

"I wanted his romantic feelings for me snuffed," she wailed. "I didn`t want to snuff out our entire friendship.

I can`t imagine my life without Harvey being part of it."

She begged the Ringmaster to help her reverse the spell.

"If you undo the spell," the Ringmaster reminded her. "Your life will be out of balance again."

Sabrina decided to take that chance.

She asked Harvey to come over to the house. While he sat on the porch bench, Sabrina forced the last of the magical scarves into his ear. PING!

With that, his memories and his feelings for her returned.

"You`ve got to let those feelings evolve," she told him. "Otherwise, we`ll never be able to move forward. "And I may never be able to move across my room."

Harvey grunted. "Easier said than done."

Sabrina didn`t get it. She`d dated other guys. What was his problem with Aaron?

"You never seemed this…serious before," Harvey explained. "I wish I could be happy for you, but I don`t think I can do this."

And with that, he left.

* * *

Sabrina returned to the Ringmaster, and told him her life was now in balance so could she please get the stupid tightrope-walking over with.

She immediately found herself back on the platform, high in the air. But this time it was different. This time… there was no safety net. GULP!

"If your life is truly in balance," said the Ringmaster. "You won`t need the net."

"Okay," Sabrina muttered to herself, beginning to cross. "Don`t look down.

Remember to breathe…" She wobbled dangerously. "Okay, don`t breathe. Almost there. Just a couple more steps…"

Which is when she slipped, and screamed as she plummeted to the floor far below!

Then somehow, she was saved by Harvey, in sequined leotards, swinging through the air on a trapeze.

"You didn`t think I`d let you fall, did you?" he asked, swinging them safely back to the platform…and then Harvey, the Ringmaster and Cirque du Sabrina disappeared, and Sabrina

discovered that her hair was now a freaky mis-coloured mess, was chasing Roxie around the house, trying to style her hair!

Then Harvey showed up, and, true to his word, Aaron greeted him warmly. He didn`t even seem to mind when Harvey had something private he wanted to say to Sabrina.

"I want you to know I`ll always be there for you if you need me," he said.

"Thanks," smiled Sabrina, hugging him. "That means a lot to me."

Harvey left, telling Sabrina, "I`ll catch you later."

As she closed the door, she smiled to herself, "And I know you always will. Hopefully, next time we won`t have to be wearing sequins."

Things finally quieted down, and Aaron and Sabrina settled in to watch a movie. When Sabrina came into the kitchen to get popcorn, she found me on the table, tied up in knots.

"Whoa!" she gasped. "Bad date with the contortionist, huh?"

"Are you kidding?" I groaned. "Best date of my life."

Sabrina laughed. "Well, you always were a little twisted."

Oh, hardy-har-har! Oof. Oh, no. Watch out. Ouch.

landed hard on her bed, her room completely back to normal.

***

Aaron came by later to apologize for acting like a jealous jerk. But it wasn`t easy to have a serious conversation.
Morgan,
having

Clowning

Oops! Sabrina's so busy juggling everything in her life, her magic has turned these poor clowns into silhouettes! Can you match up the three pairs, and find which is the odd clown out?

Around!

Blocked Off!

Sabrina's invited some of her family and friends to the circus, but her guest list is all messed up! Can you fit the 12 smaller grids into the large grid, in the right order, to spell out the names of the people she's bought tickets for?

The names to find are:

EDWARD   HILDA   ZELDA   HARVEY

ROXIE   SALEM   ARRON   MORGAN

AMANDA   DIANA

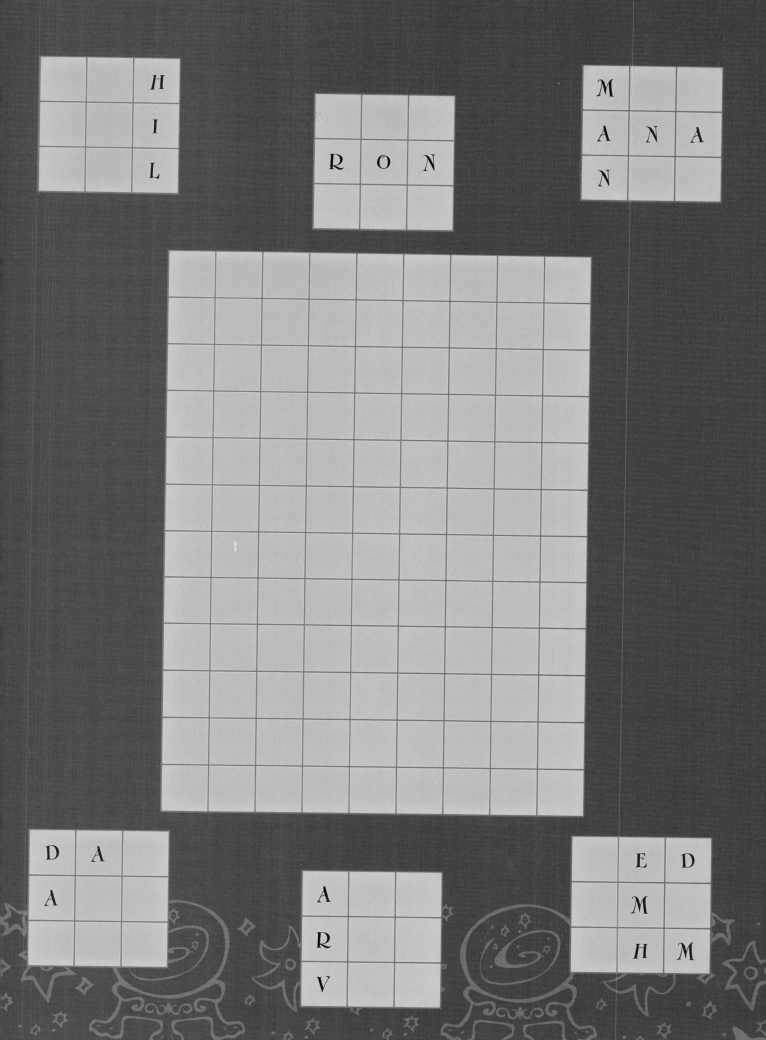

Sabrina
The Teenage
Witch™

You Slay Me

Original story written by Dan Kael

Okay people, listen up!
What is the most important day in a girl`s life? Her wedding! And guess who was planning to get married? Yes, it`s…ME!!!!!

That`s right, Aaron got down on one knee and proposed to me, and I said - - YES!!!!!

I was determined to make my day the most special - ever. (You`re invited, by the way.)

Salem and I were checking out weather forecasts on my laptop computer, trying to choose the best day for my wedding.

"Let`s see…" I said, typing onto the keyboard. "The first Saturday in June."

I hit a key - and a huge gust of wind blew me back across the room. WHOOOOSSSSH!

"Okay," I gasped, catching my breath. "Not what I meant when I said I wanted to be swept off my feet. Maybe the second Saturday…"

I hit another key. KAAA-BOOOOM! Thunder roared, and a lightning bolt struck the desk, shattering a pencil holder next to Salem. ZZZZZZ-ZZZZKKK!

"Here`s a bolt from the blue," said Salem, pawing his sizzled whiskers. "Try the third Saturday in June. Quickly."

Another key, and bright sunlight filled the room, accompanied by delightfully singing birds. Tweet! Tweet! Tweet!

"Perfect wedding day weather," I said, smiling happily.

Suddenly it began to rain - frogs!

I groaned, loudly. "I`m thinking a May wedding sounds nice."

* * *

We`d decided to hold the wedding in the back yard, exchanging our vows in an intimate setting surrounded by only family and friends.

Roxie suggested we get married au natural, professing our love, naked, under an old elm, surrounded by Mother Earth`s beauty. Forget it!

Unbeknownst to me, she and Morgan were planning a bridal shower for me. They were both expecting me to ask one of them to be my maid of honour and were ready to fight each other for the job.

I had a lot to do, and wasn`t worrying about that yet. Dress, flowers, photographer, well, everything, really. I thought I could knock off all of the preparations with one afternoon at a bridal fair. I wanted Aaron to be a part of everything, so I dragged him along with me. And yes, he turned out to be the only guy there, but he took it all in stride. You wonder why I love him?

We laughed about the big, poofy gowns and I tried one on as a joke. But the joke was on me.

"Ohmigosh!" I gasped, checking myself out in the full-length mirror. "I look like a princess." Princess Sabrina - kind`a has a ring to it!

And a princess deserved a royal wedding!

"Salem," I said, once back home and in the privacy of my room. "This wedding is going to set the tone for a whole fairy-tale life together. But without the poison apples and singing dwarfs."

I had so much to do and didn`t know where to start. I had to find a ballroom, a caterer, musicians…

"How do you even start planning a fairy-tale wedding?" I groaned. Then instantly knew. Ask a real princess.

And who better to ask than the most beautiful, the most successful, the most famous princess of them all - - Cinderella!

I pointed a finger and a pop-up cardboard

special day. You've got to insist on getting everything you want."

"I'll do that," I said. "Thanks, Cindy."

"Any problems, you know where to find me," she said. "Now, if you'll excuse me, I've got a man coming to dredge the moat." And with that, she shrank back into the castle.

Hmm. A moat. I'd like a moat!

***

So, filled with a steely determination that everything was going to be done my way for my special day, I made sure everyone knew who was in charge, including Aaron.

We'd agreed that he'd go a little non-traditional with the music and Aaron really liked this heavy metal band. I wasn't crazy about them, but since he'd let me pick everything else, I told him they'd be fine.

Then an image of Cinderella came to me.

"It's your special day, Sabrina. Insist on what you want."

I looked at Aaron. "Actually, what I meant was, no, they won't be fine."

And so it began. No one could plan my perfect wedding except me, and I let everyone know about it.

The florist, the caterer, and even the little girl allegedly an `expert` at spewing rose petals in the bride's path were all inept. I had to show them all how to do their jobs right. What ever happened to customer service?!

Back home, I was pretty insufferable, too. My two best friends *said* they'd been breaking their necks trying to give me everything I wanted but they were severely lagging behind.

"I'm surrounded by incompetents!" I yelled at them

"Who are doing the best they can," growled Roxie.

By now, neither of them wanted to be my maid of honour.

castle appeared in the pages of my magic book. A miniature Cinderella walked out of the castle, and grew to normal size in my bedroom.

"Cinderella Charming," she said, shaking my hand.

"I want to have a big fairy-tale wedding with all the trimmings," I told her. "Doves, wandering minstrels…"

"A gilded carriage with coachmen?" suggested Cinderella.

Hmm, I wasn't sure Aaron would go for that. He was planning to have his brother drive us in his minivan.

Cinderella shook her head.

"First mistake. You're the bride. This is your

"Sabrina," said Roxie, trying hard to be nice. "You`re letting this whole wedding thing turn you into an overbearing, out-of-control…"

"Monster," Morgan finished.

"Oh, please," I snorted. "You two bookends have no idea what it`s like to get married…and you never will!"

Hmph. I left them to think about that and stomped into the kitchen.

"Sabrina," said Salem, sitting on the table. "I hate to say it, but you really are turning into a monster."

I glared at him, unaware of the wisps of smoke coming from my nostrils.

"I am not a monster!" I shrieked. "I am a PRIN-CESS!"

With those words, I opened my mouth and breathed a huge ball of fire. Then I grabbed the porch doors, R-R-R-I-I-I-P-P-P-E-D them off their hinges and I stormed out of the house.

"I stand corrected," coughed Salem.

* * *

I don`t know why my friends put up with me sometimes.

But the cat has no choice, so the next day, there was Salem, sitting on a pedestal inside a changing room of the bridal fair, admiring me in my beautiful wedding gown. Unfortunately, I still wasn`t happy.

"This dress is all wrong!" I growled, fire shooting out of my nostrils.

"Hey, bridezilla," snapped Salem. "Take it down a notch!"

Outside, the saleslady asked if everything was okay?

"No, it is NOT okay!" I screamed, stamping my foot. The ground shook as if it had been hit by an earthquake!
R-R-RUUUMBLE!

"Just another raging, out-of-control bride preparing for the happiest day of her life," sighed the saleslady to her friend as they sneaked away.

"Sabrina, forget the dress," said Salem. "Look around you. Look at what you've done."

The changing room was in a shambles. Tables knocked over, dresses and veils strewn everywhere, a dismembered mannequin, smouldering boxes...

"Look under your dress," continued the cat.

"My feet!" I screamed. "And I've got a tail! And I'm leaving destruction in my wake! I'm not a princess! I'm a dragon!"

I didn't get it. Sure, I'd been the teensiest bit demanding, but I was just following Cinderella's advice!

"That'll teach you to listen to a woman who can't keep track of her shoes," snorted Salem.

"I've got to slip out of here before anyone sees me," I gasped, crashing through the outside wall of the bridal fair.

"Oh, yeah," said Salem. "Very discreet."

***

Somehow I managed to get back home without anyone seeing me...only to open the front door to find Roxie and Morgan with fifteen of my friends, all waiting to give me a surprise bridal shower!

"This is our way of saying, even though you treated us poorly." said Morgan. "We are better people than you."

To make matters worse, Aaron stopped by, too. It was way too much for me - I stomped upstairs to my room with my huge dragon feet hidden under my dress, making the whole house shake.

With everyone banging on my locked door, demanding to be let in, I knew I needed help -- fast! Opening my magic book to find Cinderella`s pop-up castle again, I rang the tiny doorbell and shrank inside.

Cinderella was in her medieval bedroom, with its beautiful canopy bed, a curved dressing table with an ornate mirror, and framed wedding photographs of Cinderella and Prince Charming everywhere. She was busy cleaning her glass slippers with a cloth.

"So," she said. "How are the wedding plans going? Found a place for the ceremony?"

"Yeah," I growled, lifting up my skirt. "Jurassic Park. Look at me. I`m a tyrannosaurus-wreck!"

Cinderella didn`t seemed fazed by the sight of me with dragon feet and tail. She said that if Aaron couldn`t accept it, I was better off without him.

"I mean, Prince Charming left me years ago," she finished. "And you don`t see me crying."

I was stunned! "He left? But I thought you had the perfect fairy-tale life?"

"No," Cinderella corrected me. "I had the perfect fairy-tale wedding." She turned to show me the etchings of the reception, and a dragon`s tail popped out from under her gown!

"You`re a dragon too," I gasped.

Cinderella smiled, dreamily. "A small price to pay for the perfect wedding day."

Then it hit me, why everything was going so horribly wrong. I had been so focused on the wedding that I`d forgotten the "happily ever after" part of the deal. I needed to go back and refocus my priorities, and pay attention to what was really important.

"Wow," I said, breathing easier. "I feel better already."

Trouble was, I still had the dragon`s feet and tail.

"You know," I said, calling out to the cosmos. "Normally when I have these revelations, the magical side-effects go away. Yo, I`ve learned my lesson!"

I checked again under my dress. No change.

"Any advice?" I asked Cinderella.

"Don`t go with the pumpkin carriage," she said. "You`ll never get rid of the smell."

Thanks a bunch. That`s the last time I take advice from a fairy-tale princess!

* * *

I got back to my bedroom, moments before Aaron climbed in through the window.

"Ahhh! No!" I screamed, hiding my tail. "You can`t come in here!"

"We`re going to talk," demanded Aaron. "Or this wedding`s off."

"But you can`t see a bride in her wedding dress," I argued. "I just saw you downstairs," he rightfully pointed out.

"And we`ve had nothing but bad luck since," I said, making him turn his back to me.

"This wedding is out of control," he muttered, staring out of the window. "This isn`t just your day, it`s our day, and I`m going to have some input."

To my amazement, Aaron`s words made my tail began to shrink!

"This whole fairy-tale wedding of yours has gone too far," he continued. "And this is one Prince Charming who is not going to put up with it anymore."

My tail shrank some more!

"Oh, of course," I spluttered. "You`re my prince."

"No," said Aaron, adamantly. "Not a prince. Just a guy who wants to spend the rest of his life with you. And you`re losing sight of that."

I nodded. "I couldn`t agree more." Looking under my dress, I breathed a sigh of relief. The tail had gone and my feet were back to normal! "All I want is the "happily ever after"!"

Aaron turned around and kissed me. "Something else we agree on," he said, holding me safely in his arms.

***

Well, after that, the wedding plans were a LOT easier. I apologised to Roxie and Morgan for the monstrous way I had been behaving, and, like best friends always do, they forgave me.

Then I told them that my maid of honour wasn`t going to be one of them! Their faces fell.

"Oh," said Roxie.

"Okay," said Morgan.

I smiled. "It`s going to be both of you!"

They screamed with delight!

"Great choice," said Morgan.

"We approve," said Roxie.

"But," said Morgan, confidentially. "I`m really the main maid of honour, right?"

She and Roxie left the room, arguing loudly. "You just couldn`t leave it alone, could you?" growled Roxie.

Shaking my head, I sighed, "Nothing is ever simple."

Upstairs, I folded up my wedding dress and put it back in its box.

"I`m definitely going with something simpler," I told Salem. "And half the petticoats. Aaron and I are just finding some middle ground. Instead of using the backyard, we found a church we like."

Salem sat on the bed, looking hurt.

"If Tweedle Dumb and Tweedle Dumber are your maids of honour," he said. "Where does that leave me?"

I stared at him, mouth open in disbelief.

"You wanted to be my maid of honour?!" I gasped.

"Well," said Salem, smiling. "It`s always nice to be asked."

What Kind Of A

Well, I was so worried about my upcoming wedding that I almost forgot to be nice to my friends! Take part in my quiz and discover what sort of friend you are!

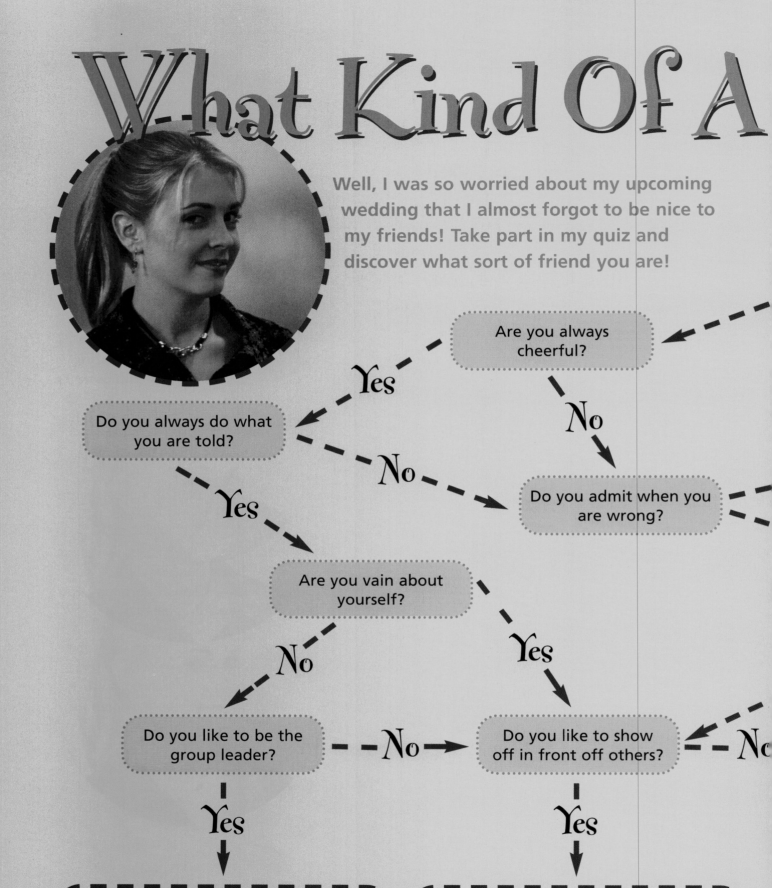

Are you always cheerful?

Do you always do what you are told?

Yes

No

No

Do you admit when you are wrong?

Yes

Are you vain about yourself?

No

Yes

Do you like to be the group leader?

No

Do you like to show off in front off others?

No

Yes

Yes

You are a natural leader with loads of enthusiasm. You are cheerful and generous and very protective of your friends.

Friends are important to you because you are a very outgoing person, but be careful you don't step on their toes and offend them by being brash and loud.

Friend Are You?

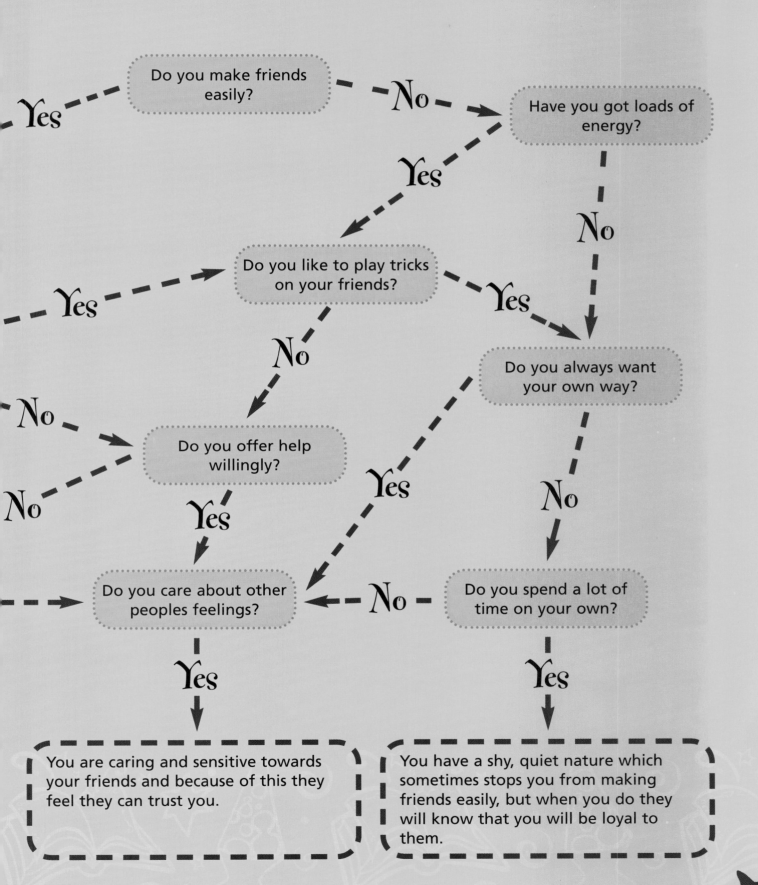

Yes

Do you make friends easily?

No

Have you got loads of energy?

Yes

No

Yes

Do you like to play tricks on your friends?

Yes

No

No

No

No

Do you always want your own way?

Do you offer help willingly?

Yes

No

Do you care about other peoples feelings?

Yes

No

Do you spend a lot of time on your own?

Yes

Yes

You are caring and sensitive towards your friends and because of this they feel they can trust you.

You have a shy, quiet nature which sometimes stops you from making friends easily, but when you do they will know that you will be loyal to them.

In A Word...

We know Sabrina's 'all grown up," but we still like to check on her from time to time (don't tell). And we're so excited she's getting married! Can you find the words listed in the grid that Sabrina needs to remember to plan a successful wedding?

The words can be found horizontally, vertically, diagonally...and even back-to-front! One word is listed twice!

The words to find are:

BELLS
BOUQUET
BRIDAL SHOWER
BRIDE
BUFFET
CATERER
CHURCH

EXCHANGE VOWS
GIFTS
GROOM
GUESTS
HONEYMOON
MAID OF HONOUR
MUSICIANS

PHOTOGRAPHS
RECEPTION
RINGS
ROSE PETALS
VEIL
WEDDING CAKE
WEDDING GOWN

R	O	S	E	P	E	T	A	L	S	C	R	B	A	R
E	I	T	T	E	F	F	U	B	H	W	E	R	L	E
C	S	N	A	I	C	I	S	U	M	L	R	I	F	W
E	X	C	G	A	Y	P	R	H	L	B	E	D	K	O
P	K	V	O	S	Z	C	N	S	P	V	T	E	Q	H
T	R	A	B	P	H	O	T	O	G	R	A	P	H	S
I	H	T	C	L	S	T	G	O	H	J	C	V	O	L
O	X	I	D	G	Y	B	O	U	Q	U	E	T	N	A
N	W	O	G	G	N	I	D	D	E	W	P	T	E	D
S	V	E	N	G	A	I	J	M	E	S	V	B	Y	I
M	A	R	R	C	I	Q	D	X	B	P	T	O	M	R
R	U	O	N	O	H	F	O	D	I	A	M	S	O	B
T	O	F	G	U	E	S	T	S	E	L	A	K	O	E
M	Y	L	I	M	A	F	R	S	U	W	T	L	N	M
E	X	C	H	A	N	G	E	V	O	W	S	K	R	A

Answer: The word listed twice is Gifts

A Fish Tale

Original story written by Adam Englan

Salem here again, cat fans! (Hey, this is a story about a fish - who else is gonna tell it?)

Well, Sabrina`s wedding plans were going as smoothly as they could, under the circumstances. Having quit her job at Scorch Magazine, she had become a successful freelance writer, with lots of job offers.

And she and Aaron had decided to move to Los Angeles after they were married. Roxie and Morgan, although heartbroken at the thought of losing their best friend, were busy trying to find a new roommate to live with them. (Soft-hearted Sabrina had told them they were welcome to stay at her Aunts house and rent out her room once she had left. Personally, I`d have charged them double.)

"Don`t worry," she told me, after they had gone out to put up flyers advertising the spare room. "I have an Other Realm contractor coming to disconnect the portal...and your vocal cords." (She was kiddin`! I think!) "Now there won`t be any more magical surprises popping in."

Which is when thunder and lightning could be seen and heard coming from the living room. KKRRAAKKAADOOM!

"Like that," groaned Sabrina.

***

This magical surprise turned out to be her nasty, bitter, twisted (and those are just her good points!) Aunt Irma. (She`s a witch, in both senses of the word.)

"Aunt Irma," said Sabrina, trying to fake a smile. "What a pleasant…what a lovely…what a surprise."

"It shouldn`t be!" snapped Aunt Irma. "I believe there`s something you`d like to share?"

"Not really," lied Sabrina. "I mean, I`ve switched shampoos, bought a couple new tyres, I`m getting married…"

"That`s the one," said Aunt Irma. "Congratulations!"

Sabrina was dumbstruck. Her Aunt Irma didn`t have any problems with her getting married to a mortal? No death and destruction? No plague of scorpions?

"You know where I stand on witches marrying mortals," said Aunt Irma. "But if you insist, I suppose that Harvey Kinkle is the least offensive of the lot."

Ahh…! She didn`t know, then.

"I`m not marrying Harvey!" spluttered Sabrina.

"So who is this mystery groom?" demanded Aunt Irma. "He is a witch, isn`t he? Because if he`s not…"

She pointed a finger. Thunder and lightning erupted again, smashing a vase on the mantel. KKRRAAKKA-SMASSH!

Sabrina swallowed hard. "I can tell you this," she stuttered nervously.

"Aaron`s mother is a real witch. And his father`s a bit of a gnome."

"Splendid!" cheered Aunt Irma, satisfied. "I must meet the boy."

Meet Aaron? Not what Sabrina wanted - at all. But she had no choice...so she invited him to dinner for Aunt Irma`s approval.

***

Aaron arrived with a bouquet of freshly picked daisies to get on Aunt Irma`s good side.

"She has no good side," Sabrina warned him. Aunt Irma`s a nut. Correction. She`s a kook. Check that. She`s insane. Whatever she says, play along and don`t question her."

"Sabrina, calm down," Aaron said reassuringly, staring into her eyes. "I`m sure I can handle your aunt. "When`s she getting here?"

"Now," said Aunt Irma, suddenly sitting next to Aaron.

"Whoa!" said Aaron, jumping in shock. "Where`d you come from?"

Aunt Irma smiled. "The Big Dipper."

Aaron frowned, but remembering what Sabrina had said, he replied, "Oh, I love it there."

Aunt Irma was quite surprised. "Do you visit the outer reaches often?"

"I think I am right now," said Aaron, stifling a giggle. "I mean," he hastened to add. "Just last week I was backpacking on Mars."

Sabrina`s Aunt told him that her sixteenth husband had died in a backpacking accident on Mars. "Fortunately for me," she cackled. "They never proved a thing." Yeeps!

To make Aunt Irma think Aaron really was a witch, Sabrina discreetly pointed her finger, making it look as if Aaron had magically created a sumptuous meal on the dining room table! PING!

"What manners," beamed Aunt Irma, as Aaron put her arm in his and led her to the table. "And such manly magic."

***

Meanwhile, Roxie and Morgan were interviewing prospective roommates at the diner. It wasn`t going very successfully - Roxie had found something wrong with every applicant.

"I`m sorry," said Roxie, after she`d turned down yet another girl. "But no one is ever going to measure up to Sabrina." (Well, she`s got that right.)

Then Betty, a waitress at the diner, said she was looking for a room.

"Betty, huh?" said Morgan, hopefully, knowing the right answer would give the woman a chance to win Roxie`s approval. "Is that short for...Bettrina?"

"No, said Betty.

Oh, well. Nice try, Morgan.

Back at the house, Aaron`s charm was winning over Aunt Irma. When she told him she was over one thousand years old, he didn`t even blink - he just said she didn`t look a day over five hundred.

"You have quite a catch there," Aunt Irma told Sabrina. "And...you have my blessing."

Woo-hoo!

It was then that Roxie and Morgan turned

nice oil

Thinking her troubles over, Sabrina went back to the living room…and found Harvey talking to Aunt Irma.

"What are you talking about?" he was saying. "Aaron's not a witch."

Aunt Irma turned on Sabrina. "You lied to me!" she hissed.

"Lied? No," said Sabrina. "All I did was deliberately mislead you at every possible turn. But in my defence, you did say Aaron was quite a catch."

"That's true," agreed Aunt Irma, pointing a finger towards Aaron, who was sulking in the dining room because Harvey had turned up. "I did."

PING!

They all hurried into the dining room, where Aaron had now turned into a fish, swimming around in a small fish bowl.

"And now he's the catch of the day," cackled demented Aunt Irma.

Sabrina groaned. "So," she asked, heart sinking. "Do we still have your blessing?"

*　*　*

Boy, was Sabrina ticked off at Harvey.

"You're single-handedly destroying my relationship!" she hissed at him.

Aunt Irma chimed in. "Don't be angry at Harvey. You only have yourself to blame."

"I'm sorry if my choices don't fit with your warped world view," Sabrina said angrily to her aunt. "But it doesn't give you the right to do this."

Aunt Irma seemed to think she had every right.

"Listen, you mean, vindictive crone," Sabrina yelled. "You're not going to get away with this. I am going to do whatever it takes so Aaron and I can walk down the aisle. She glanced over to the fish bowl. "Or, swim, as the case may be."

Grabbing the fish bowl, Sabrina stormed out, marching into the kitchen where I was dozing.

up with Betty to check out the room. Morgan was still trying to convince Roxie that Betty was a perfect replacement for Sabrina.

Sabrina, panicking, hustled them upstairs before they ran into Aunt Irma. "Remember, you can't make a decision on a place until you've slept in it," she told a confused Betty. "Don't come down until you've had a good night's sleep."

"Imagine her as a blonde," Morgan was saying to Roxie, pointing at Betty. Then she asked Betty, "Ever thought of dyeing your hair?"

"This better be some room," muttered Betty, already thinking this was a crazy house.

*　*　*

"Oh, boy!" I purred, instantly awake. "A goldfish! Can I eat him?"

"That's Aaron," said Sabrina.

"So," I asked, licking my lips. "Is that a yes or a no?"

* * *

Harvey came in, looking apologetic.

"Sabrina, I'm so sorry," he said. Yeah, sure he was! "I didn't do it on purpose, I swear. Besides, you know I always thought there was something fishy about him."

Harvey laughed. Sabrina didn't. She told him to watch over Aaron while she tried to fix the mess. Hurrying upstairs, she collided with her roommates and Betty.

Morgan was desperately trying to get Roxie to accept someone as their new roommate, and kept pitching the "Betty is just like Sabrina" angle.

"You guys are going to have to wear name tags for me to tell you apart," she laughed.

Betty looked at Morgan and groaned. "Is she part of the deal?"

"It's negotiable," snorted Roxie.

Sabrina didn't have time for this! She ran into her bedroom, slamming the door. Her magic book opened to a page with a telegraph machine and she tapped out a Spellman family alert.

Then Harvey entered, holding up two kittens.

"Say hello to Roxie and Morgan," he said. "They startled Aunt Irma, and she doesn't have much of a safety on that ping finger."

Sabrina groaned. "Where's Aaron?" she asked. Harvey told her that Betty was watching him.

"What?" she screamed, rushing out of the room. "You left a strange women and a hungry cat with my fish? I mean, fiancé!"

And Sabrina had good reason to be worried. Trying to fill the fish bowl with fresh water, Betty had accidentally poured poor Aaron down the drain!

Sabrina sent Betty outside to watch the kittens, then pointed at Harvey and herself. PING! They were inside the kitchen pipes.

You've heard that curiosity killed the cat? Well, in this case it just sucked him down the drain.

***

Before I knew it, we were all inside a revolting sewer system, wading through stuff you don't even want to imagine! Uck! Sabrina and Harvey were holding tiny fish nets, while I was armed with a fishing rod.

"Great," groaned Sabrina. "Most marriages end up in the sewer. Mine's starting there. Why is this so hard? It's like the entire universe is conspiring to keep us apart."

Suddenly, my rod started bending. "Hey, I think I've got something!" I squealed.

But whatever it was, it wasn't Aaron. While Sabrina was bossing me around about how to reel him in, Harvey had fished up Aaron in his net. Sabrina hadn't seen this, and Harvey debated what to do...but not for long.

"Harvey!" cheered Sabrina, noticing the goldfish. "You found him! Thank you, thank you, thank you. I don't know what I'd do without you."

Harvey sighed, sadly. "I think you'd do just fine."

"Wait a minute," I said, still struggling with my line. "If you've got Aaron, then...what've I got?"

Well, whatever it was, it pulled me into the stinking water. SPLOOSSH!

Sabrina giggled. "A long bath coming."

***

We returned home to find that Aunt Irma had turned Betty into kitten number three. Sabrina demanded that she turn Aaron back to normal. Of course, the old battleaxe still refused to let Sabrina marry a mortal (or a fish) Aaron.

"Fine," said Sabrina, angrily. "Then you leave me with no choice."

And with that, she emptied all the magic inside her into a crystal vase.

"I'm giving up my magic," she told Aunt Irma. "You can't object to two mortals getting married."

Aunt Irma snorted. "Guess what? I can and I do. So get rid of your magic, stomp your feet, slam the door, but I'm not turning him back."

Sabrina would not relent. I`ve never seen her act so tough. Especially against an old witch as powerful and touchy as Aunt Irma.

"If it takes me the rest of my life, I will marry this fish!" she declared, before storming upstairs with Aaron in a plastic bag.

Aunt Irma looked at Sabrina`s magic inside the vase.

"Harvey," she said. "How`d you like to be an all-powerful being? What would you say if I offered you Sabrina`s magic?"

Harvey refused.

"Oh, come on now, Harvey," purred Aunt Irma. "Are you telling me there isn`t something, or..." She glanced upstairs. "Someone that you desire? Magic can make many things possible."

She`s mean, but she`s perceptive. I`ll give her that.

Harvey stared at the vase of magic. This could be his last chance to win Sabrina for himself...!

* * *

In the bathroom, Sabrina was sitting on the edge of the tub, flicking through her magic book. Aaron was swimming around in the bath, which Sabrina had filled with cold water.

"I`ve got to say," she told him. "You`re holding up pretty well under the circumstances. And you`re really a great swimmer."

It was then - PING! - that Aaron turned human again! He sat up in the tub,

soaking wet and
very confused!

"What`s going
on?!" he sputtered.

"You, uh, fainted," said
Sabrina, quickly.

Aaron glared at her in disbelief. "So
you put me in a bathtub with all my clothes on?"

"You`d have done the same for me," said
Sabrina, tossing him a towel. "I`ll be back. "And
with that, she ran back downstairs.

Aunt Irma was putting on her coat, getting
ready to leave.

"Obviously that boy loves you very much,"
Aunt Irma told her.

"He really does," Sabrina said, thinking
Aunt Irma had turned Aaron human again. "And
if you`ll just give him a chance, you`ll understand
why I love Aaron, too."

Aunt Irma stared at her. "Aaron? I`m
talking about Harvey. I gave him the powers of
the universe - your magic, actually."

Sabrina was dumbstruck! "Harvey changed
Aaron back? Why couldn`t I do that?"

"You were trying to undo my spell,"
explained Aunt Irma. "He was trying to make you
happy. Turns out his was a much more powerful
motive."

"I can`t believe he did that for me,"
Sabrina gasped.

Before leaving, Aunt Irma relented and
told Sabrina she could marry Aaron, although she
still wasn`t happy about it. She also turned Roxie,
Morgan and Betty back to normal.

"What`s going on?" spluttered Roxie, as
they found themselves around the dining room
table in front of saucers of milk.

"I don`t know," fumed Betty. "But you two
are freaks!" And with that, she stormed out.

***

Sabrina hurried to Harvey`s apartment to thank
him, only to discover that he was gone!
His apartment was completely empty, except for a
box in the middle of the floor. Inside it was
Sabrina`s vase of magic. As she lifted it up, the
magic swirled back inside her. WHOOSSH!

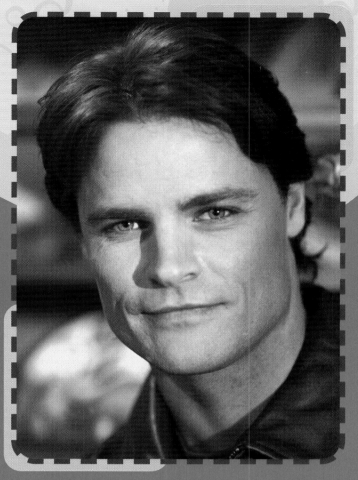

There was a note in the bottom of the box.
It read, "May your life be filled with happiness
and with the magic only you can create. I`ll always
love you. Harvey."

Sabrina looked around the empty room,
stinging tears of sadness swelling in her eyes.

"Goodbye, Harvey," she whispered.

***

Back home, Morgan and Roxie were shocked to
discover that Harvey had left.

"I can`t believe he`s really gone," said
Roxie.

"Neither can I," said Sabrina.

"So he just cleaned out the entire
apartment?" asked Morgan.

"Just up and left it vacant, huh?" said
Roxie, as she and Morgan ran for the door. Maybe
Harvey`s apartment would be a cheaper option!

"It`s already rented," Sabrina told them.
"Betty got it."

Oh, well. Win some. Lose
some. Hee-hee...!

Gone Fishin'

You will need:

A thin stick or garden cane
Cotton or thing string
Five A4 sheets of thin card
Tracing paper
Coloured paints or felt pens
Sticky tape
Scissors
A small magnet (from craft shops)
Ten paper clips
A large cardboard box

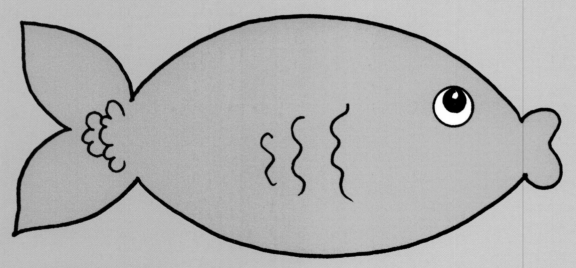

1 Trace the fish shape on this page onto the card ten times (two fish shapes per card) and cut them out. Colour them in, and write a number on each fish 1-9. One of them mark with a large `A` for Aaron!

Mee-ooow! Rotten Sabrina wouldn't let me eat her new fish...just because it was Aaron! If you'd like to play this great fishing game, just follow the instructions!

2 Take the stick or cane and tie the cotton or string to one end. Tie or stick the magnet to the other end to make your fishing rod.

3 Stick a paper clip on the back of each fish. Decorate the box with your paints or felt pens to make it look like a fish tank. (You might also want to decorate it with seashells and glitter.) Put the fish into your tank.

How to Play

This is a game for two players. Taking it in turns, use the magnetic rod to pull a fish out of your tank. If you pull out the `Aaron` fish, you miss a turn and have to throw it back. Keep going until all the fish have been caught. Whoever pulls out the fish with the highest score is the winner!

Say Cheese!

Since I wouldn't let Salem eat Aaron, I made him some cheese fish. That cat has the life. He tries to eat my fiance, and still gets a treat! If you`d like to make some for your friends (or your cat), follow the instructions below. Ask a grown-up to help!

You will need:

85g of grated cheese
2 eggs
225g of plain flour
100g of butter or margarine
Pinch of salt
Pinch of dry mustard

1 Sieve the flour, salt and mustard powder into a bowl. Cut the butter into very small pieces with a rounded knife and add to the bowl. Rub the mixture with your fingers until it becomes like breadcrumbs.

2 Take the eggs and break them into a separate bowl, whisking them with a fork. Add the eggs and grated cheese to the flour mixture and knead the mixture together onto a pastry board into a ball.

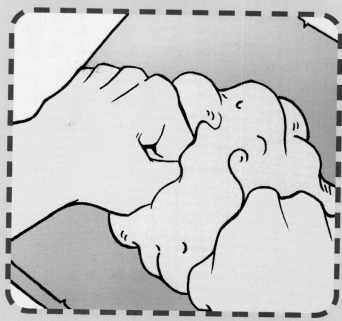

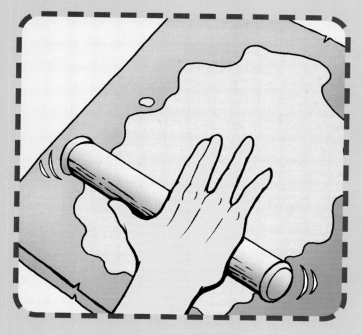

3 Taking a rolling pin, roll the pastry onto a flour-covered pastry board until it's roughly 6mm thick.

4 Carefully cut out the pastry into fish shapes and put them onto a greased baking tray. Ask a grown-up to put the tray into a pre-heated oven (Gas Mark 6/425F/220C). Leave to cook for 8-10 minutes until golden brown.

5 When ready, you can either eat them hot as a main meal, or cold as a snack!

Soul Mates

Original story written by Dan Berendsen

This was it. The greatest moment of my life. My wedding day!

So of course it started with me…oversleeping. Luckily, Salem was on hand to wake me up with a blast of his tuna breath. Gross!

"Can you believe it?" I sighed, sitting up in bed. "I`m actually getting married today. Woo-hoo."

Salem taunted me.

"So, how do you feel?" he asked. "Nervous, frightened, scared, tense, petrified…?"

"…excited, happy, joyful," I answered. "I`m getting married. How do you think I feel?"

But Salem was wondering if I was getting cold feet. Would I actually go through with the wedding?

"Salem," I snorted, swinging my legs out of bed. "I do not have cold feet."
THUNK!

I looked down to find my feet encased in a thick block of ice.

"See?" I gulped nervously. "They`re not cold." I let out a low moan. "They`re frozen solid!"

* * *

Downstairs, panic reigned. Morgan and Roxie were still not dressed, and nothing was ready.

"What`s going on?" demanded Aaron, arriving with his mom and dad. "Why aren`t the flowers at the church? Why aren`t you ready yet?"

"Aaron, don`t worry. We`ve got it all under control," Roxie lied.

"Under control?" scoffed Morgan. "I still have to do my hair, my nails, and my make-up has to be perfect. Some of us don`t have the option of wearing a veil."

"Ohmigod!"

screamed Roxie. "I still have to steam Sabrina`s veil."

And then they both remembered that neither one of them had woken me up yet.

They rushed up to my room, to find the floor covered with ice that I had spent the last fifteen minutes chipping off my feet.

"It just occurred to me," I said quickly to

their puzzled reaction. "That I might not have ordered enough crushed ice for the reception."

Morgan reminded me that I needed something, old, new, borrowed and blue for luck.

"Don't worry," said Roxie, as they rushed out again. "We'll take care of it."

It was then that my teenage witch cousin Amanda appeared from nowhere.

"I'm so happy for you," she squealed excitedly, giving me a hug.

I started to put up my hair, telling Amanda that I was in a kind of a panic and not to get in the way.

"What's with her?" Amanda asked Salem.

"She's having second thoughts," he said.

"No second thoughts," I snapped. "Maybe

just some regrets...that so many people I love can't be here. My mom is in Peru. You never know about my dad. And I have no idea why my aunts haven't R.S.V.P.'d."

Amanda asked if Harvey would be at the wedding. Ouch!

"I'd love for him to be there," I sighed sadly. "But...he just can't be. You're too young to understand."

It was then that Aaron yelled for me to get downstairs - quickly! Now what?

* * *

Aaron was in the living room with my Aunt Hilda. And her wedding present to us - a llama!

"Cut me some slack," she said to a shocked Aaron. "There's not a lot you can pick up in Peru. It was this or dysentery."

Peru? She must have seen my mom. I had to get the scoop. Telling Amanda to chat with Aaron and his family - and chat only, no pointing - I rushed Aunt Hilda and the llama into the kitchen.

"So how did my mom look?" I asked eagerly. "What did she say?"

"Why don't you ask her yourself?" chuckled Aunt Hilda, pointing her finger at the llama. P!NG!

The llama changed into my mother, Diana Spellman!

"I can't believe you're here!" I gasped, hugging her tightly. "And you're not a ball of wax."

Time out: For those of you who don't know, my dad's a warlock who married mom, a mortal. This really peeved off the Witches' Council who had this rule that after I got my witch's

powers, I couldn`t see my mom again or she`d turn into a ball of wax.

"You can thank Hilda and Zelda," mom explained. "They took me before the Witches' Council and pleaded my case."

"Every mother should be at her daughter`s wedding," Aunt Hilda said.

I was delighted...until I realised Aunt Zelda wasn`t with them. But she was. Aunt Hilda took a large candle out of her purse and set it down on the table.

"You know the Witches' Council," she said. "There`s always a trade off." Poor Aunt Zelda. But at least it was only until after the wedding.

"This is the greatest gift ever," I told Aunt Hilda. "I can`t believe it. All of the Spellman women together again."

Then I noticed it seemed awful quiet in the living room.

"Wait. Where`s Amanda?" I asked.

***

Good question. The answer to which had just magically appeared - PING! - on the back of Harvey`s motorcycle as he drove it down a country road. VRROOOM!

Startled, Harvey crashed his bike into a hedge. SMASH!

"Surprised to see me?" Amanda asked, watching Harvey pushing his now-mangled motorcycle out of a ditch.

"Not at all," he fumed. "I wanted to test my new engine by ramming it into a tree."

Ignoring Harvey`s sarcasm, Amanda told him she had come

to take him to my wedding, telling him that I wanted him there.

"She does?" he gasped excitedly. We hadn`t seen each other since he`d saved Aaron from being a fish. Then his face grew dark. "Well, that`s too bad. It`s not going to happen.

"Why not?" demanded Amanda.

"You`re too young to understand," he said.

"I really wish people would quit saying that," Amanda sniffed.

***

Meanwhile, I had a few problems of my own. Doubt had crept in. No, really, he had. I found him sitting on my bed, eating a packet of peanuts.

"Apparently," he said. "There`s some serious doubting going on around here."

"No," I answered. "No doubt. The man I love is downstairs. I`m getting married."

Doubt pulled a small jewellery box from his pocket. "Guess I went all the way to the North Star for nothing," he told me, handing over the box.

Inside was a beautiful stone that radiated light like a small star. I could see Aaron smiling up at me from inside the stone.

"This is his soul stone?" I asked. "Why are you giving me this?"

"Because isn`t that what you`re doubting? Whether or not you and Aaron are soul mates? If it`s truly meant to be," Doubt said, pointing to a jagged edge on the stone. "Your pieces should fit together perfectly."

Which meant I now had to rush to the North Star, somewhere in the middle of the galaxy, to get my own soul stone! Like, I didn`t have enough to do already?

But I had to go. I had to know.

So one quick `ping` to the North Star later, I put the two soul stones together, and...they didn`t fit!

Well, they almost fit together. There was an image of me and Aaron together in the stones, but we couldn`t reach each other.

"Oh, no!" I groaned. "What am I going to say. "I almost

do?""

***

This was crazy. I did love Aaron. I was certain of it. Well, almost certain. But I didn`t have time to think about it. I was already late for my own wedding.

Rushing to the church, dressed in my beautiful wedding gown, I slipped into the bridal chamber, locked the door and pointed up a grinding wheel in front of me.

While the guests were waiting impatiently in their pews for the bride to appear, I tried desperately to grind down the edge of one of the stones, to make them fit. It was hopeless.

In the end I gave up, slipping the stones into a small bag hanging from my wrist. I loved Aaron and he loved me. We were practically soul mates. What more could I want?

It seemed like the whole church came in to see what was keeping me. Aaron took charge. Gotta love that, right?

"I`d like to have a moment with Sabrina," he told everyone.

"You can`t be in here," Morgan cried. "You can`t see the bride in her wedding dress."

"But if I don`t," he said. "I`m afraid there might not be a wedding."

Well, that cleared them all out.

Aaron could tell I was anxious and nervous and he said he was having doubts, too.

That helped a little, but I had to ask him. "Do you think we're...soul mates?"

Aaron frowned. "Soul mates? You mean, are we destined to be together? Sabrina, life doesn't have any guarantees. All we can do is try to make each other happy. The one thing I don't doubt is that I love you."

"I love you too," I answered. And I did. But...No, don't go there, Sabrina.

"So," he asked tentatively. "Should we do this?"

"Absolutely," I beamed. "And remember, when you see me, act surprised."

***

Roxie and Morgan were waiting for me at the back of the church, Salem looked very handsome in his little tux, watching from a perch. As Roxie painted one of my toenails blue, Morgan gave me five dollars she had borrowed from a flower girl, and a new phone number she had just got from the best man.

All I needed was something old and I was ready to be an official bride. Morgan came to the rescue again.

"And a bracelet I grabbed out of your jewellery box," she said, fastening it around my wrist. "Which makes it old and stolen."

"You look so beautiful," Roxie said, slipping the veil over my face.

This was it. I really was getting married.

Then I noticed that someone was missing - again. "Where's Amanda?" I asked.

She came running out of the bridal chamber, looking slightly guilty.

"Sorry. Just had some business to take care of," she said. I frowned at her. "You're too old to understand," she chuckled.

Hmm...

***

While last minute nerves were jangling in my stomach, half-way across town Harvey came out of a store to find a small jewellery box on the seat of his motorcycle. Puzzled, he opened it...

***

Amanda, and then Roxie and Morgan, walked down the aisle as the wedding procession began. Salem took this moment alone with me to give me his present.

"Listen," he said, pushing an envelope towards me. "Don't get all weepy on me, but I got you a little something."

That was so sweet. I opened the envelope.

"Cash?" I gasped.

"Salem." Then I read the notes attached to the cash.

""Happy sixteenth birthday...Happy seventeenth."

You've been stealing my

birthday card money all these years?!"

Genuine tears swelled up in Salem's eyes.

"And I promised myself," he sniffed sadly. "I wouldn't cry."

Before I could think of anything to say, another surprise appeared.

"Anyone looking for a father of the bride?" he chuckled.

"Dad!" I squealed in shock and delight, looking at my father, Edward, in front of me. "I can't believe you made it."

I slipped my arm though his...and then noticed the bracelet Morgan had put on my wrist.

"Ohmigod!" I cried in alarm. "I can't wear this!"

My dad took it off my wrist. "12:36?" he asked, reading the engraving.

"Harvey gave that to me seven years ago," I explained. "Twelve thirty six is the exact time we met."

I looked at the bracelet and then down at the aisle, where Aaron was waiting nervously at the altar. Oh, no! What should I do?

***

I called mom and Aunt Hilda to the back of the church to give me some much-needed advice. I explained about the circus, and the fish thing and the soul stones not fitting together.

"No more," my mom answered.

"No more what, no more?" I asked, aware that I'd stopped making sense somewhere around the goldfish.

"Magic," she said. "So two pieces of glowing coal don't fit together. Who cares? What matters is what's in your heart. No magic can tell you that."

"Your mother's right," agreed Aunt Hilda. "Sabrina, whatever you decide, it's not the end of the world."

I looked down the aisle at Aaron. And made my decision.

"You two are the best," I said, giving them both a hug. "Tell everyone I'll be right there."

As the first chords of `The Wedding March` struck up, I slipped my arm back in dad's, and walked towards my destiny...I was going to marry Aaron!

***

"Sabrina," said the minister, facing me and Aaron at the front of the church, all

eyes glued on us. "If you`d like to begin."

"Okay." I took a deep breath. "I, Sabrina Spellman, take Aaron Jacobs to be..."

And that`s when the bag fell off my wrist and onto the floor, one of the stones rolling out. I scrambled to put it back in the bag.

"Sorry," I apologised to a puzzled Aaron. "Where was I? Oh, yeah. I, Sabrina Spellman, take Aaron Jacobs to be my partner in life, my one true..." I hesitated, unable to speak the most important word of all! I looked down at the bag. "My one true...my..."

I couldn`t do it! I couldn`t go through with it. There is no `almost` in soul mates. By now, Aaron knew exactly what I was thinking and feeling.

"You`re such a wonderful guy," I told him, after pulling him to one side so we could speak in private.

"But we`re not too halves of a whole," he answered.

He smiled, understanding. "Sabrina, all I want is for you to be happy. If we`re not soul mates, we shouldn`t be doing this."

I felt so rotten! "Aaron, I am so sorry," I said.

He put his arms around me.

"Don`t be. Never think that almost is good enough for you."

"Or for you," I whispered, holding back the tears. We gently kissed, one last time...

***

With the church in an uproar at Aaron`s

announcement that the wedding had been cancelled, I hurried outside for some fresh air.

Pulling off my veil, I was amazed to see Harvey at the curb, leaning on his motorcycle.

"I don`t exactly know what this is," he said, holding up a soul stone. "But something tells me I`ll find the answer here."

I took my soul stone from the bag. "And I think I just found mine," I said, walking down the church steps towards him. He took me in his arms and kissed me. It felt so right. Aunt Hilda, Amanda and Salem came out of the church, Hilda holding Aunt Zelda the Candle.

"It`s about time," they all chorused together. And Aunt Zelda`s wick lit up!

Slipping on the motorcycle behind Harvey, I held on tight as he pulled away, both of us tossing our soul stones over our shoulders. They rolled together to form one perfect stone. Clearly seen on the new stone was an image of me and Harvey kissing.
The other guests crowded onto the steps to watch us go.
"I guess that`s the something old she needed," Roxie said to Morgan, laughing.

My dad looked at his watch. "Would you look at that?" he said to Aunt Hilda. "Twelve thirty-six on the dot."

Love Is In The Air!

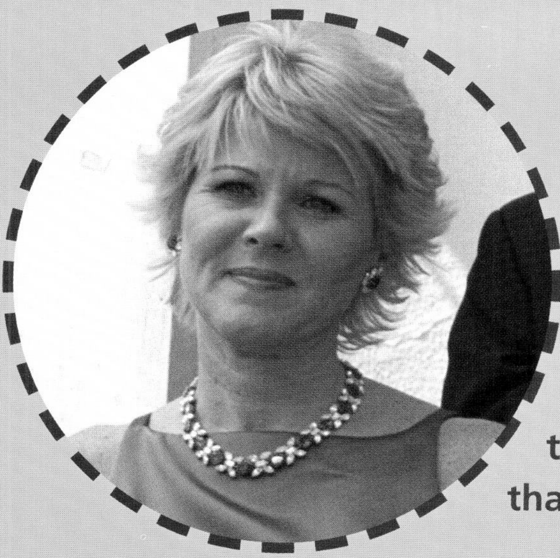

Well, in the end, Sabrina didn`t actually get married, but I`m sure she will - one day! Can you unscramble the letters in the Soul Stones to find out the names of family and friends that Sabrina loves?

1 M A S L E

3 D H I L A

4 R M A N G O

2 L E D A Z

7 E D A D W R

6 H V R Y E A

5 D N I A A

8 X O E R I

Answers:1) Salem 2) Zelda 3) Hilda 4) Morgan 5) Diana 6) Harvey 7) Edward 8) Roxie

Designing Sabrina's Wedding Gown!

Hey, everyone! I want YOU to help me design my next wedding dress! (Harvey and I will tie the knot, hopefully very soon!) You can colour in my dress with coloured pencils or crayons, and decorate it with sticky shapes or glitter sticks. (Just remember not to shut the annual until the glue has dried!) Afterwards, colour in the picture!